T0114896

THE TRUE REPLACEMENT SON

Dorothy Audrey Simpson

WestBow Press books may be ordered through booksellers or by contacting:

WestBow Press
A Division of Thomas Nelson & Zondervan
1663 Liberty Drive
Bloomington, IN 47403
www.westbowpress.com
844-714-3454

ISBN: 979-8-3850-0188-0 (sc)
ISBN: 979-8-3850-0189-7 (e)

Library of Congress Control Number: 2023912117

Print information available on the last page.

WestBow Press rev. date: 06/29/2023

AUTHOR'S NOTE

The persons, places and the events portrayed in this novel are fictional. Any resemblance to real people or incidents is not intended and is purely coincidental. This story is a work of fiction; hence, names of characters, places and incidents are the product of the author's imagination--except for actual historical figures as in Biblical references. With the exception of prominent historical places, persons, and incidents, any resemblance to actual persons--living or dead--or to events or locales is entirely coincidental. Scriptures cited are from the *King James Version* of *The Holy Bible.*

CHAPTER 1

"YOUR FIFTH NOVEL, LARRY! AND on the *New York Times* best seller list! You're going on television talk shows! Are you sure you want to marry me--just an unknown English literature professor at a small university? A nobody!" Barbara was ecstatic about Larry's success.

"A nobody? You're the most important person in the world, Barbara! I couldn't live without you! I couldn't write without you! And yes, we are going to be married, the sooner the better! Then we'll buy a nice house some place around here--a house with a white picket fence, a swimming pool--everything you want!"

"You only came out to Colorado to get some peace and quiet in a beautiful setting so the muses would bless you! Are you sure you don't want to move back to New York?"

"You're my favorite muse!" Larry grinned.

"A muse from Pueblo, Colorado?"

"I don't care if you're from Timbuktu! You're going to be my wife and my muse from now on!"

Lawrence Carpenter, known as Larry, was thirty, dedicated to his writing profession. He and Barbara had dated several years. It was time to tie the knot. Barbara's parents had died in a house fire when she was in her early twenties. Lawrence's parents were touring Europe.So it was a small wedding, with only a few friends attending.

They spent their honeymoon at Lake Tahoe. Then they bought a new home in a small town in southern Colorado where Barbara taught English literature at the college and Larry started working on a new novel.

Larry's lanky figure towered above his wife. He was six feet four inches to her five foot four. Larry was not a handsome man. His big ears stuck out sideways so much so that his classmates had always teased him, said they could hang their hats on his ears. His thin neck showed a sharp "Adam's apple" which bobbed when he talked. He was so thin that his college friends had called him "scarecrow." And his thin hair was already beginning to recede.

Barbara was an attractive 28 years of age with blond hair and deep-set blue eyes. She was petite where Larry was tall and gangling. Barbara did not marry Larry for his "looks." His appearance made no different to her. She loved his intellectual nature. She loved his writing ability. And she loved his fame and fortune. He was known around the country as one of the best writers of the decade.

Time seemed to fly for the newlyweds. Larry looked at the calendar one day and realized their first anniversary was coming up. He immediately called and made reservations at a special restaurant in Denver. They needed a night out to celebrate.

The dinner was fabulous. Over dessert Barbara seemed a little nervous. Larry was sensitive to his wife's moods. She had no reason to be nervous--none he could think of. Finally, Barbara said, "Darling, I have to tell you something."

Larry's heart sank. Was she having an affair with another professor at the college? Did she want a divorce? Was she going to resign from her position? What could it be?

"We're going to have a baby," she said.

"You're pregnant?" Larry spoke so loudly another couple at a nearby table turned to look at them. Larry lowered his voice. “That’s wonderful, Darling! It’s what we’ve been hoping for! When did you find out?”

“A couple of days ago. I wanted to wait and tell you on our anniversary.”

“Aways the romantic,” Larry said softly. “I couldn’t be happier! I think this is the happiest moment of my life!”

“I thought the happiest moment was when your publisher said you might win the Pulitzer Prize!”

“Moments like that pale in light of something like this! Sweetheart, let’s go home and bask in the joy of anticipating the greatest event in our lives--the greatest after our marriage, of course.”

Barbara was pleased that Larry was so delighted. They had talked about having a baby soon after they were married. She thought life was perfect. Little did she know that sometimes sorrow follows joy.

CHAPTER 2

BARBARA WAS MISERABLE THROUGHOUT THE entire pregnancy. The nausea and vomiting lasted longer than all her "pregnancy books" told her it should. Her weight gain was much more than the guidelines recommended. Her feet were swollen. She felt like a walrus. In the last months she could hardly sleep. There was no comfortable position.

Larry sympathized but felt helpless. When Barbara went into labor, Larry rushed her to the hospital, hoping for a quick delivery. But Barbara was in labor for twelve hours. She moaned and yelled and cursed Larry the whole time. In the last stage of labor, she screamed at the doctors and nurses. Larry stood by helplessly, wondering when the nightmare would end.

Finally, their son was born. Barbara's mood changed immediately. She and Larry beamed with happiness as they viewed the beautiful baby boy.

"Let's name him Alan after your father," Larry suggested. Barbara was pleased with the name.

The birth of their son was the height of happiness for the Carpenters. Barbara recovered quickly and loved every moment of nursing her son. Larry took dozens of photos and sent them to everyone he could think of, telling them that he was the proud father of a boy named Alan. The child had curly, blond hair and blue eyes. Never had parents been so attentive, so happy, so fulfilled.

Larry's books continued to fly off the shelves. His fifth novel had over a million copies sold, and he was working on a sixth. Barbara was a proud stay-at-home mother and wife.

Alan was precocious. Larry took hundreds of pictures of the boy as he developed first one skill, then another, walking well before the average age, talking with a good vocabulary when he was still in diapers. When Larry and Barbara were alone, Alan was the main topic of their conversation.

"He's going to be a writer like you," Barbara said.

"Or a professor like you," Larry replied.

"Only better!" Barbara exclaimed.

"Oh, he will be better than both of us. After all, he is the product of both of us."

"We are so fortunate to have him, Larry," Barbara mused. "I don't want another child. I don't want him to have to compete for attention, for resources, for anything. I want him to have all we have to give him, exclusively, totally his own."

"An only child needs to learn to get along with others. That's why having siblings helps a child learn to share, to make friends, to be socially well adjusted," Larry argued.

"I don't care. I won't share Alan with anyone, not even a little brother or sister."

"Whatever you say, Darling," Larry agreed. "It makes no difference to me. I want Alan to have the best of everything, just as you do: the best education, the best resources. He will never lack in having the best love any parents could give."

As they watched Alan grow, their pride grew with him. No one had a better son. No one had a smarter child. He was obedient. He learned quickly. He was handsome. He had not inherited his father's awkward body or his father's ungainly features. His ears were a little big, but Barbara knew he would "grow into them." Alan was neither too thin nor too plump. At four years of age, he had a perfect little body, skilled fingers, sharp eyes, and an alert mind.

When Alan was five, the Carpenters decided to buy a new home--one with a larger yard for Alan to play in. They could get him a puppy. They would have a swimming pool and teach the boy to swim. It was a dream home.

They had been in the new home three months when Alan had his fifth birthday on June tenth. What a party Barbara planned for him! Friends brought their children.

"It's time for cake and ice cream!" Barbara told the little group. They gathered around the table where a beautiful cake was topped with five candles. Barbara lit the candles.

"Blow out your candles, Alan. Be sure to make a wish first!"

Alan blew them out with delight.

After having cake and ice cream, Alan opened his gifts and was delighted with them. One of the gifts was a little fire truck.

"I'm going to be a fireman when I grow up," Alan exclaimed.

"You can do whatever you want when you grow up, Son," Larry assured the boy.

Then the adults sat by the pool while the children played in the enclosed front yard under big shade trees, including a big old weeping willow. Roses were blooming around the yard and gave off a delicate fragrance.

"You're lucky to have a pool," Lucy, a good friend, told Barbara. "These Colorado summers are short but can get hot."

"Don't I know it!" Barbara replied. "We've always wanted a pool. Larry likes to take a swim every morning on those hot days. And he's going to teach Alan to swim. Alan thinks he can swim already! He's always been able to learn everything quickly. We had to tell him he'd have to wait for his daddy to teach him."

"Children learn fast," Lucy exclaimed.

"Larry wants to spend more time with Alan now, so there will be lots of swimming lessons. Larry's new novel is released next month. We're having a big celebration on July 25th," Barbara told the group. "We want you all to come."

She was assured that the friends would be there to help celebrate. And they were all there on that fateful day in July.

CHAPTER 3

THE HOT JULY SUN SHOWN down on the Carpenter's home as guests arrived to celebrate Lawrence Carpenter's new novel. This time the adults did not bring their children, so Alan played alone in the front yard, enjoying the little fire truck he'd received for his birthday. The adults had drinks by the pool. Barbara could hear Alan making various noises as he played with his truck.

"Larry is building a greenhouse in the back," Barbara said proudly. "Do you want to see it? It will be beautiful once he finishes the job."

The group of adults all affirmed that they did.

"Come on, Larry. Show the folks your newest project!" Barbara urged her husband. "He's only been working on it since the beginning of the month. And here it is the 25th and he's almost done!" Barbara extoled.

The group left the pool area and went to the back of the property where Larry had started building a very small but efficient greenhouse. As Larry explained some details to his friends, Barbara noticed it suddenly seemed very quiet in the yard.

"Excuse me. I'm going to check on Alan," she said as she left the group. She went back to the pool area to go through the gate to the front part of the yard. As she approached the pool she wondered what she saw in the water. And then she screamed. Alan was floating face down in the pool!

Everything was a blur after that: Larry retrieving Alan from the water; the sirens; the EMT's working over Alan's little body; the hospital; and, finally, the doctor's grim expression when he came out of the emergency room to tell them: Alan had drowned, and nothing could have saved him. Somehow, the gate from the front yard to the back pool area had been left open. They had always been careful to keep that gate shut. Alan must have gone to the gate to call his mom or dad and pushed it open.

The days were a blur after that, black, bitter, filled with indescribable pain for the grieving parents. Nothing could help. They tried grief counseling. It didn't help. They travelled out of the country, even took a cruise. That didn't help. Months went by and their grief was like a suffocating blanket, one they could not throw off.

Barbara refused to change anything in Alan's room. She wanted everything left just as it had been that fateful July day. She had placed Larry's little firetruck, his favorite toy, on a table near the bed. Nothing else had been changed or moved.

One day Larry found Barbara sitting in Alan's room, just staring at the wall.

"Sweetheart, don't you think it's time to...to move on...give these things away," Larry suggested, pointing to Alan's closet.

"No!" she expelled a heavy breath.

"He's not coming back," Larry said gently.

"I know that! But this is all I have left of him! You don't believe in God. I think I do, but I don't know if I believe in heaven. I want to think that Alan is in heaven. But I just don't know. How can we know for sure? How can we know anything for sure? I hear people say it's all in the Bible. They say to believe! But what? How?"

"No one can know anything. The Bible was written by men and is full of contradictions. You won't find answers there or anywhere. We have a life and when it's gone, it's gone for good. We can't bring Alan back. We have to move on," Larry said.

"You say that. But I have Christian friends who tell me God takes children to heaven when they die. They tell me Alan is in heaven. I want to believe; but I never read the Bible or went to church like my friends have. I don't know what to think!" Barbara dissolved into tears.

Larry held her in his arms a long time.

"I've been thinking about something," he said after her sobbing had abated.

"What, Larry?" she managed.

"We could have another child."

"No! Never! I won't go through having another baby!" She exclaimed. "Besides, no child could take away the grief we have over losing Alan."

"OK, Honey, OK," Larry said calmly.

Barbara noticed that her husband had aged in the last weeks. His hair line seemed to be receding more than ever. There were small lines in his face.

"Then what if we adopted a child?" Larry suggested. "You wouldn't have to go through pregnancy and childbirth. We could get a baby and he'd take your mind off of...things...and I think it would be good for us."

"Maybe," she conceded.

"Let's think it over," he said.

"But he can't have this room!" Barbara snapped.

"No, he'd have his own, new room," Larry said. "We have that extra guest room. That could be converted to a child's room."

"Maybe I'd like that," Barbara said. "A new baby, a boy....".

CHAPTER 4

With Larry's famous name and his generous income, the Carpenters had no trouble at the adoption agency. There were not many babies available, however. They considered adopting an older child, but they truly wanted a baby, a boy.

Finally, they were called and told there was one baby boy that needed a home, but it wasn't certain he could be adopted. The woman on the phone asked the couple to come in to discuss the possibility with her.

The women in charge, Nancy Pierce, seemed hesitant. "He hasn't been adopted because...well...we're hoping the couple will take his twin sister, as well. Most couples only want one child. But we'd like to keep these twins together," the woman at the desk told them. Mrs. Pierce was a young, heavy-set woman with long, dark hair. "In fact, the birth mother insisted that they be adopted together, never separated. And I don't know what she'd do if we didn't adopt them out together."

The anxious couple wanted to see the boy. With dark brown hair and blue eyes, the baby was nothing less than gorgeous.

"We want him," the Carpenters said in unison.

"And his sister?" Mrs. Pierce asked hopefully.

"Surely you can find another couple to take the girl, can't you, Mrs. Pierce?" Larry asked in reply.

"Well, yes...." Mrs. Pierce said, disappointment in her voice. "But the birth mother will not be happy about separating the twins. She was very insistent that they be kept together. She could cause problems if her wishes were not carried out."

"Why does she have to know?" Barbara asked.

"I suppose she doesn't," Mrs. Pierce conceded. "There are ways," she mused.

"Why does anyone have to know?" Larry echoed. "Can't you give us a birth certificate just showing the boy's birth?"

"The existing birth certificate showing two live births would have to be changed. The State wouldn't do that. It would be false."

"But there are ways to get it done," Larry said. "You must know that."

"If I were a dishonest person, yes, I know of such ways," Mrs. Pierce said.

"I know you're an honest person, but you can help us out, can't you?" Larry said, taking ten hundred-dollar bills from his billfold. He placed them in front of Mrs. Pierce. "I know it would cost something to get a new certificate showing only the boy's birth," Larry said. "But if you can manage it, we'd be very grateful. Of course, there would be a change for the baby girl, too. Maybe if the birth mother thought the boy had died, she wouldn't question the adoption of the girl. The birth mother doesn't have to see the boy's certificate. And the girl's certificate could show the birth of twins where the boy died."

Nancy Pierce hesitated. "There's more where that came from," Larry indicated the bills. "After we get the proper certificate."

"I'll see what I can do. I'll call you when the certificate is ready," Mrs. Pierce said, taking the bills from the desktop. "I'm sure you'll want to show your gratitude at that time."

"Absolutely," Larry said. "See you soon!"

After they got into their luxury vehicle, Barbara asked, "Why is a birth certificate so important, Larry?"

"I want the boy to grow up thinking he is an only child. If he knew he was a twin, he'd want to know why we didn't adopt his sister. Also, the birth mother could cause a great deal of trouble if she knew we didn't take the girl. This way, the birth mother will think the male twin died. Someone will adopt the female. No one will be hurt by this. The boy's modified certificate will show a single, live birth. The other certificate, which will go to the people who adopt the girl, will show that twins were born but the male died. Whoever adopts the girl will be happy, and we'll be happy. Our son will know he's adopted but he doesn't have to know he had a sister. And his twin sister will never know she has a living brother. All we need are the proper birth certificates."

"But isn't there something illegal about that, Larry?" Barbara questioned.

"Making a minor change like that? What's the big deal? No one cares," he replied. "It's not like we're producing counterfeit money or something."

Barbara laughed. "You don't need to make counterfeit money, Larry. The way you keep bringing it in from your book sales, you could pay off the national debt!"

"Well, not quite," Larry replied. "But close," he chuckled.

Larry answered the telephone one morning and was surprised to hear from Nancy Pierce so soon. He and Barbara stopped by the adoption agency immediately and saw Mrs. Pierce at her desk. She had the altered birth certificate, showing that the baby boy had been born "a single birth."

"No one is going to know or be hurt because of this, isn't that right, Mr. Carpenter?" Mrs. Pierce asked.

"You can rest assured of that," Larry answered. "You took care of the girl's certificate, too?"

"Of course," the woman replied. "Your son's certificate shows a single birth. As for the girl's certificate, it still shows the birth of twins, a girl and a boy, but with a little modification," she paused. "It now shows that the male did not live. That way the birth mother won't have any objections."

"Did the payment I gave you last week cover the cost?"

"Well, just about," Mrs. Pierce answered slowly, with a slight smile.

"This should do it then," Larry said, slipping another thousand dollars into the woman's hand.

"It certainly will," Mrs. Pierce assured him. "Another couple is going to adopt the baby girl--a doctor and his wife. She'll have a good home."

"That's good!" Larry replied.

Later when they were home, Larry told Barbara to keep the boy's birth certificate in their safe deposit box at the local bank.

"I feel kind of bad about not taking the two babies, like the birth mother wanted, but we really only want one child," Barbara said. "Just a boy."

"The birth mother won't even know. Mrs. Pierce took care of it. I think she just wanted a good home for the additional kid, trying to talk us into taking two instead of one. You'd think we were adopting a puppy or something. We just wanted a boy and that's what we got," Larry replied.

He was right. The adoption papers were in order and the Carpenters brought home their adopted baby—Eric--the next day.

While they still mourned for Alan, the Carpenters discovered that having a new baby in the home took their minds off their sorrows. As Eric grew, they took pleasure in his progress, just as they had as Alan had developed. Eric was smart and agile, just as Alan had been. But he seemed unhappy. He cried a great deal. He sobbed in his sleep. As he grew older, he had nightmares.

Then he grew rebellious. He didn't readily obey his parents' commands as Alan had done. He seemed to like to cause trouble, throwing food on the floor so Barbara would have to clean it up or refusing to dress in the clothes he was told to wear.

"I wish he'd be more like Alan," Barbara said more than once. "Alan never caused trouble. He always obeyed without question."

"Well, every child is different," was all Larry could say.

One day Eric discovered the "secret" room--the unchanged bedroom that had been Alan's. There were toys in there. Eric went in to play with them. Barbara spanked him when she discovered he'd gone into the room and started playing with Alan's toys.

"I want to play with the little firetruck!" Eric exclaimed.

"No! You can't touch that firetruck!" Barbara screamed, pulling Eric away and slamming the bedroom door shut. "You can never, never go into this room!" she yelled. "They are your brother Alan's things. You can't touch them!"

Larry had just come in from running some errands when he heard Barbara.

screaming.

"Barbara, how can you expect Eric to understand?" Larry said after Barbara explained.

"Talk to him, Larry. Tell him about Alan. Tell Eric how we adopted him and want him to be our son now."

Larry explained to Eric about Alan's death and how Barbara kept the room just as it had been. "After Alan died, we were so sad. He died in a swimming pool when we were having a party. Someone left the gate open, and....Well, then afterwards, that's when we found you. And now we're happy again," Larry told Eric. "You needed parents, and we needed a child, so we adopted you. But you must not go into Alan's room again. Your mother wants to keep it just like it was, and we must respect her wishes."

Barbara had Larry put a lock on the door so Eric couldn't get in again.

As Eric became more difficult, Barbara, in exasperation, would scream, "Why can't you be like Alan? He always obeyed immediately! He never questioned! What's wrong with you?"

Even Larry would find himself thinking of Alan when he tried to teach Eric something to which Eric objected and resisted.

"Alan would have jumped at the chance to learn this!" Larry would say. "If your brother Alan hadn't died—"

"Well, he did die, and I'm not him!" Eric yelled.

Eric's grades in elementary school were good. But when he entered middle school, his grades dropped. The teachers said Eric was smart but "lazy." He didn't put forth an effort. He barely did enough work just to get by. In the eighth grade, Larry and Barbara confronted Eric about his grades.

"Eric, you're smart. Your test scores show you're way above average in intelligence. Why are your grades so low? Your mother and I worked hard to get through college and make good incomes. You won't get into college if you don't bring your grades up!" Larry admonished.

"Who said I wanted to go to college? I'd just as soon drop out of school and get a job," Eric replied.

"What job? What can you do to earn a decent living without a college education?"

"It might interest you to know that not everyone in the world goes to college, and they live just fine," Eric retorted.

"The teachers say you're lazy, Eric," Barbara said. "And I agree. You won't even make your own bed!"

"Where's the rule that says you have to make your bed every morning?" Eric replied.

"I made the rule!" Barbara retorted.

"Well, I don't think you're exactly the queen of the world," Eric said.

"Eric! Show more respect for your mother!" Larry demanded.

"You mean Barbara? She's not my mother," Eric said, "And you're not my father."

"We adopted you!" Barbara insisted. "That makes us your parents!"

"No one told you to. You didn't have to. It's not my fault if you adopted me."

Barbara sobbed quietly, exasperated.

"Now you've upset your mother," Larry accused.

"Like I said, she's not my mother," Eric said, making an ugly face.

"Don't talk like that!" Larry exclaimed.

"Make me stop! Go ahead, kill me! You never wanted me! You just wanted me to replace your dead son. You couldn't keep him alive because you were too busy partying with your friends! Don't blame me for your dead son--and don't expect me to take his place."

Eric went to his room and slammed the door.

Barbara dissolved into tears. Larry held her in his arms, seething in anger.

Eric was extremely handsome, what some would call "movie-star" handsome. He knew it, and he used his looks to his advantage. He was slim and tall, about six feet in height when he was in the tenth grade. He had dark brown hair, straight, white teeth, dimples when he smiled, perfect skin tone, and his body was tall and slim. His blue eyes were deep and compelling, framed with dark lashes. Some of Eric's teachers would "give him a break" just because he was the son of Lawrence Carpenter--and the fact that he was so good looking didn't hurt. So when Eric deserved an "F," he was often given a "D" or even a "C."

Larry tried to get Eric interested in sports. But Eric insisted he had no interest in any athletic events. Barbara tried to get Eric into several activities, but Eric had no interest. They tried to interest in him band, in theatre, in choir, in art classes. The boy had no ambition. He was lazy. The teachers were right. Throughout high school, Eric continued to do just enough "to get by," making grades of "D" most of the time.

One day Barbara yelled at Eric in her frustration at his failing grades. "Why can't you be more like Alan?" she cried.

"Maybe I would be if I was dead!" Eric retorted.

He was tired of competing with a perfect ghost. As a living boy, he made mistakes. His older brother was perfect, of course--because he was dead.

Eric's parents had high aspirations for him. He should be an outstanding success like his parents, even famous like Larry. Eric just wanted to be left alone. As Larry and Barbara became more and more disappointed in Eric, the youth became more and more apathetic. His grades were good enough to earn his high school diploma--barely.

After his high school graduation, Larry wanted Eric to go to the college in their small town. Even with his poor grades, the community college would accept him. But Eric applied for a job at the local hardware store and got it. He was happy enough to earn his own money, thinking he would get an apartment and move out of the house as soon as he could.

"You are throwing away a good opportunity to go to college and have a career," Larry told him.

"You can't force me to do anything I don't want to do," Eric retorted.

Later, Eric thought to himself, "Sure, they've provided for me, and they can cut me off of their funds any time. I don't care. I can support myself now. They never loved me anyway. I was just a substitute for their son."

And then he met a lovely girl—Darlene--and his world changed.

CHAPTER 5

ERIC WAS WORKING AT THE hardware store when a customer came in with a list. She was the most beautiful girl he'd ever seen! She was tall and slim, had blue eyes and golden blond hair. The hair was long, down to her waist. And when she smiled at Eric, he noticed dimples in her cheeks.

"My father sent me with this list," the girl said. "Can you help me find these things?"

"Oh...oh, yes, of course," Eric managed. He wanted to get to know this girl. After he had her purchases in a bag, she gave him a check, signed by her father.

"Dr. Bill Simms," Eric said, looking at the check "Is your father a doctor?"

"Yes, he's a surgeon at the hospital," she said. "We've only been here a few months. We moved down from Denver. My mother was tired of the big city. She was brought up in a small town and missed living in a place like this. We're very happy here. Oh, I'm Darlene Simms."

"Eric Carpenter. It's nice to meet you, Darlene. And you...go to school?"

"Yes. I'm enrolled at the college," she said. "This is my first semester."

"I'd like to see you again," Eric said. "Would you have coffee with me at Brown's Cafe?"

"I'd like that," she smiled.

"Well, I don't work tomorrow. What time are you free from your classes?"

With a time and place decided on, the two went their separate ways. There was definitely an attraction.

In the weeks that followed, Eric and Darlene spent every spare moment together. They were amazed to discover how much they had in common. They liked the same movies, the same books, the same types of music. Darlene mentioned that she had been adopted.

"You're adopted?" Eric was surprised. "Did you know I'm adopted, too?"

"You're not kidding? I never knew!" Darlene exclaimed. "We do have a lot I common!"

One day over lunch at Brown's Café, Darlene said, "Tell me about your folks."

"My dad's a writer, as you know. He always expected me to be some famous intellect like him, but I don't want to be famous. I just want to be a regular guy."

"And your mother?"

"She's never gotten over the death of their son, Alan. She's always compared me to him. So did my dad. They sent me to a counselor once when I was in middle school. I was rebellious, and I guess they thought a counselor would straighten me out. The counselor was nice. He told me he understood it must be hard to complete with a dead child. He said I was "a replacement son."

"A replacement son?" Darlene asked.

"He explained that my parents probably wanted me as a replacement for the son that died. The trouble is, they think of Alan, my brother, as being perfect, and I can't measure up. How can I compete with a ghost?" The counselor understood, but he had no answers for me.

"It isn't fair. My parents never had children. My mom couldn't. So that's why they adopted me," Darlene said. "I didn't have to replace another child."

"You're lucky. When I was little, I thought I was loved. Later, I realized I was adopted to be a substitute or replacement for the son that died. I know my parents care about me, but I know they don't love me the way they loved Alan."

"That must have been a rough childhood," Darlene sympathized. "I have to say that I had a happy childhood. My parents have been wonderful. But I've always been curious about my birth parents. Haven't you wondered about yours?"

"Sure. Maybe one of these days I will look them up. Larry and Barbara are very hush-hush about it. They don't even want me to talk about being adopted."

"Oh, my parents are pretty open," Darlene said. "But they don't know much. They do have some details which would make it easy for me to find out more. I've just never got around to it."

"I don't know anything about my birth parents," Eric said. "But we're adults now. We can make our own life, our own happiness. And that's what I intend to do."

The romance between Eric and Darlene deepened as the weeks went by. Darlene was making good progress in her studies to become a nurse.

Eric proposed to Darlene one evening.

"I don't have a ring, but if you promise to marry me, someday I'll buy you the biggest diamond you've ever seen," he said.

"I don't want a diamond ring. I just want you! I would be so proud to be your wife," Darlene replied.

Eric took Darlene into his arms and held her for long moments. Finally, she broke away and sighed. "How will we manage? You know I'm living at home while I'm in college, and you're still living at home until you can get out own your own. We don't have the money for our own apartment yet.

"My parents smother me," Eric said, "Especially Barbara. She doesn't want me to be independent. They would give me the money for an apartment, I suppose. But I don't want to have to ask."

"I could quit school and get a job," Darlene said.

"No. I want you to have that nursing career you want--and that takes an education," Eric insisted. "We'll just have to wait until I can save up enough for an apartment."

Weeks passed and the young couple grew more and more in love. Darlene took Eric home to meet her parents--Bill and Judy Simms. They approved of Eric. His good looks did not hurt anything; and his father's reputation as an author made Eric a "good catch."

"But he doesn't have a career," Judy complained later to Bill. "Working in a hardware store! He should be in college! His dad is brilliant! And they have plenty of money. They could send him to any college he'd choose."

"I think he's just trying to find himself," Bill replied. "It's hard for a young person to be expected to follow in a famous parent's footsteps. He's still young. I think he'll be OK."

"Well, you're the doctor," Judy smiled. "I'm sure you're right. Anyway, Darlene seems happy and that's the most important thing."

Eric also introduced Darlene to his parents, and they approved of her. "She's smart and she has ambition!" Barbara commented later she was alone with Eric.

Meaning that I'm not, Eric thought to himself. But he held his tongue.

Finally, Eric and Darlene just went to a Justice of the Peace to get married. They didn't want "any fuss" as Eric said. He had bought some inexpensive rings. "They're just for now," Eric said. "I'll buy you an expensive ring later," he promised.

Darlene knew they could not afford a big wedding, nor would their parents approve of their marriage before Darlene finished school. So they took the plunge. They announced their marriage the next day.

Bill and Judy Simms seemed happy. A big, elaborate wedding would have been nice, they thought. But perhaps the happy couple had made the right choice, they decided.

Eric's parents were fairly indifferent. However, to show their support, Larry and Barbara gave the young couple a car for a wedding gift. They also agreed to pay the rent on an apartment until Eric could afford it. Darlene's parents wanted to help, too. They agreed to pay all the utilities until the young couple had more income.

"We don't want charity," Eric said. "We'll accept the help for now--but we're going to pay you back as soon as possible."

"That's right," Darlene agreed. "I'll keep track and we'll pay back every penny."

Sometimes Eric took Darlene over to his family's home where they could enjoy a big screen television and barbecue food outdoors. When Larry was traveling on a book tour, Barbara often accompanied him. Then Eric and Darlene had the big house to themselves in return for "housesitting" and caring for the two dogs. They enjoyed the time together as they took walks or enjoyed the garden. The swimming pool had been filled in after Alan's death and the area had been made into a rose garden.

Eric told Darlene about the "secret room" which was still just as it had been when five-year-old Alan had died.

"They locked it up so I wouldn't go in there and play with the toys when I was little. But I could see it through the outside window. Barbara keeps it just like it was the day Alan died.

"That's kind of morbid, isn't it?" Darlene asked.

"Kind of! But what can I say? I'm just the replacement son."

They told themselves they would always be together. They would someday have a home or their own, not just a small apartment. And they would always be happily married. Nothing could separate them as a couple. Or so they thought. But there was one thing that could.

CHAPTER 6

Darlene graduated as a Licensed Practical Nurse and immediately obtained a job at the local hospital where her father worked. Eric had been promoted to manager of the hardware store. They could now afford to pay their own expenses and made monthly payments to their respective parents for the help they'd been given.

Life was good. One evening after dinner, Darlene cleared the table and lit some candles.

"What's the special occasion?" Eric asked.

"I know we don't have a lot of extra money and won't have until we have our parents paid off. But we have enough, don't we?" Darlene asked.

"Enough? Yes, we have enough. What are you thinking? Enough to buy a house? Probably not yet--but soon," Eric said.

"We can put off buying a house," Darlene said. "How about enough for a baby?"

"A baby? You mean you're...you mean--" Eric was speechless.

"Yes!" Darlene beamed.

"I couldn't be happier!" Eric exclaimed. He took Darlene into his arms and gave her a tender kiss.

After some time, the happy couple announced the news to their parents. Darlene's parents were delighted. Eric's parents were a little subdued but said they were happy. Eric figured they probably thought the young couple couldn't afford a baby yet. But Eric would make sure they had enough to support their child.

"I don't want you to work while you're pregnant," Eric told Darlene. "I have a friend with some extra weekend work I can do. We'll have enough. I want you to take it easy until our child is born--and then stay home until he or she is old enough for kindergarten."

"I'd like that, Eric, but I don't want you to kill yourself working all those extra hours."

"I'll enjoy the work, knowing it's for you and our child," Eric said.

Darlene resigned and stayed home, working on making a small room into a nursery. She also started going to a church near their apartment. She came home one Sunday and told Eric she had made a commitment to Christ. She had heard the gospel message of salvation and had accepted Jesus as her personal Lord and Savior. She had been born again, as explained in the third chapter of the gospel of John. She was going to be baptized the next Sunday.

"That's wonderful, Darlene, if that's what you want. I'm an agnostic, so I won't usually go to church with you; but I'll go to see you get baptized," Eric promised.

"Eric, I wasn't brought up in a church. My parents believe in God. They go to church on special occasions. But they never talked to me about a personal relationship with Christ. I learned about Him in church. I wish you'd listen to the gospel message and accept Christ as your Savior."

"I can't believe there's a God when so many bad things happen in the world."

"Well, God doesn't cause the bad things. The devil causes all the bad in the world."

"I don't believe in the devil, either," Eric said. "Or heaven or hell. I think we make our own heaven or hell here on earth; and then we die and that's it."

"Well, if you will listen to the gospel message and read the Bible, you might change your mind," Darlene said gently. "Jesus said in order to enter heaven, you must be born again. That means believe in Him and commit your life to Him. I wish you'd read the third chapter of John."

"OK," he said. "I'll get around to it. Let's talk about it later, Eric said.

One evening Darlene announced that she had been doing some checking on her birth parents. "I want to know what genetics our child will be inheriting," she said, "from our birth parents. We need to find yours as well as mine. I've located my birth mother and I'm going to call her tomorrow. She lives just outside of Denver. Then we'll look to find your biological parents."

"I agree it would be good to know our genetic background for the sake of our child," Eric said. "I'll see what I can find out from Larry and Barbara, but they've never been open to talking about my adoption, much less my birth mother."

Eric went to the Carpenter's home the next day. He and Larry sat outside and drank iced tea. Eric asked his dad about the adoption details. Larry was reluctant to tell Eric about his adoption.

As he sat there, Larry remembered the day they had gone to the agency to adopt a child. He remembered the woman at the desk, a young, heavy-set woman with long, black hair--Mrs. Nancy Pierce. He remembered what she'd had said when Larry and Barbara had told her they wanted to adopt the baby boy. They had been approved for adoption and had seen the baby. They thought he was perfect for them.

"There's just one thing," the woman behind the desk had told him. "He has a twin sister. The birth mother requested that the twins be adopted together. Would you want to take the girl, as well?"

"No, we only want a boy," Barbara had said.

"Don't you want to at least see the girl?" the woman, Mrs. Pierce, had asked.

"No. We aren't interested," Larry had insisted. "We just want the boy."

Mrs. Pierce had sighed and turned to some paperwork. It was then that Larry realized that it would be advantageous to have a couple of birth certificate changes. It would avoid problems with the birth mother.

Eric had never known he had a twin sister. Barbara had never wanted to talk about the adoption, and Larry wanted the deception regarding the birth certificates to remain a secret. They had wanted to protect Eric from any kind of concern about his adoption. But now it was time. Eric was an adult. He had a right to know. He told Eric the name of the adoption agency, that he had paid for some changes.

"Eric, we never told you this. But you had a twin sister. We didn't adopt her because we just wanted a baby boy. But the girl went to a good family, we were told. Mrs. Pierce was the woman we worked with. She assured us that the girl would go to a good family."

"What? I have a twin?" Eric exclaimed. After a pause, he shouted, "Why didn't you tell me?"

"It just never came up, never seemed important," Larry shrugged.

Eric stalked out of the room, slammed the door, got into his car and drove home.

When he got to the apartment, he found Darlene washing dishes.

"So what did you find out?" she asked.

"I'm a twin! They never told me! Can you believe my self-centered parents never even told me I had a twin sister? How could they adopt me without her? How could they separate us? It's wrong! Just wrong!" he fumed.

Darlene tried to comfort him but without much success.

The next evening Darlene told Eric she had talked to her birth mother on the telephone-- a woman named Jacqueline Tompson. She was married to Wayne Tompson, and they had two children. She had seemed glad to hear from Darlene. She had been willing to talk to

Darlene about the circumstances of her birth. But she seemed to want to keep it quiet. She said she'd had twins, a boy and a girl. She had been told the boy had died.

"I don't think her husband or children know she gave birth before she married. I think she kept it a secret. She was probably ashamed." Jacqueline had given Darlene the name of the adoption agency. "My name was Jacqueline Baker then," she had explained.

"It turns out the same adoption agency had handled both of our adoptions," Darlene told Eric. "You'll be able to find out something about your birth parents," Darlene assured him. "I have sent to the State for our birth certificates."

CHAPTER 7

One morning Darlene went out to shop for baby clothes. She met a friend for lunch so did not get back to the apartment until afternoon. She had left a sandwich for Eric, as he usually took an hour off to eat lunch with her.

When she entered the apartment, she knew something was wrong. Eric was lying on the sofa, a bottle of whiskey sitting on the floor beside him. Eric never indulged in alcohol. He might have some champagne on a special occasion, but that was about it.

"Eric? Eric, what's wrong?" Darlene was at his side. She shook him gently.

"Whatza-matter? Shu never seen sumnun drunk before?" Eric slurred.

"Eric, this isn't like you! You've never missed an afternoon of work before! What will happen to the store? They depend on you!"

"Don' leckure me," Eric said.

"Eric, I want to know what's going on! Why did you miss work? Why are you drinking whiskey?"

After getting Eric to drink some coffee and supervising a shower, Eric sat with a towel wrapped around him, another cup of coffee in front of him, along with a piece of cake Darlene insisted he try to eat.

"Please Eric, tell me what's going on!" Darlene said, sitting across from him.

"Oh, everythin's jest fine," he said. His speech was a little better and he seemed able to sit at the table without falling over. "I jest foun' out my ol' man and my ol' lady..."

"Please, Eric," Darlene pleaded. "I know they didn't tell you that you were a twin. That was wrong. And they should have adopted your sister along with you."

"Thatz right," Eric said. "Our birth certificates...from the State.... came in the mail. Now looka those paperz an' tell me why I shouldn't jest kill myself right now."

"Kill yourself? Eric! You know that would be wrong! So wrong!"

"Jest read 'em," he insisted, pushing the papers toward her.

Darlene looked at the birth certificates sent by the State. The birth certificate for Eric showed a single birth of a male. But the birth certificate for Darlene showed that she was a twin, born with a brother, a baby that had died.

"What does this mean?" she mused. "I knew I had a twin brother who died. But I don't understand."

"My wunner-ful dad explained it all to me. I talked to him on the phone a while ago. He admitted that he paid the worker at the agency to change my birth certi....certificate, to show I was a single birth, but I really had a twin sister," Eric managed.

"I still don't understand," Darlene said.

"'Couse you wouldn't. My good, ol' dad didn't want me to know I had a twin sister. The lady he paid off. . . .paid off. . . changed the certificates. 'parently the lady told your parents you had a twin brother that died right after birth. Turns out you and me. . . . we're the twins. We got the same birth mom. Same parentz. The woman was paid to show that the boy had died. That was me....And I didn't die. So now you see...whatz the purpose of livin'?"

"Why? How?" Darlene was confused.

"Look at the two certificates," Eric said. He seemed to be somewhat sober now. "Same birth mother, Jacqueline Baker. Same date of birth. Only one shows only a single male birth. The other shows twins; but the boy died. The girl—that would be you—lived. The boy that died--that would be me. 'cept you ken see I'm not dead."

"So Jacqueline Tompson—Mrs. Wayne Tompson—was Jacqueline Baker back then," Darlene said. "I need to pray." She felt the blood drain from her face. She almost fainted. She had to sit down and put her head down below her knees. She took deep breaths.

"Prayin' won't change anythin'. We gotta get a divorce. And you gotta git an abortion."

"Right now we need to get hold of ourselves. You need to get sober. And I need to lie down before I faint."

Darlene fell onto the bed in their bedroom. The shock was too much for her. She was so stunned she couldn't think. She could still see the lines on the birth certificates.

Eric entered the room behind her and fell into a chair by the bed. "Gotta find another place to sleep," Eric mumbled. "We're twins! I married my sister!"

"Oh, Eric!" Darlene sobbed.

"You're my better half, all right!" Eric said. "My sister, my wife!"

CHAPTER 8

THE NEXT MORNING THE COUPLE had recovered enough to discuss the problem they now faced.

"When I talked to my dad before, he told me I was a twin, but they didn't want to adopt my twin sister. I was so mad, I left. I didn't want to listen to him. Yesterday on the phone he told me that he'd had the certificates changed. He probably didn't want the birth mother to object if the twins weren't adopted together—so they listed the boy as a dead--and the girl would be adopted with no one any wiser. Then he changed my certificate to show a single birth of a male. I've heard my dad say some things in the past about not wanting to adopt a girl. I've heard some things my parents said when they didn't know I was listening. It didn't make sense before, but now it does."

"Well, we know the name of the adoption agency, so maybe we can find out something more there," Darlene said. She still refused to believe what the certificates declared. "There must be some mistake."

"I doubt it, but we can try to find out more," Eric said.

"And we can talk to our birth mother to see if she knows anything more about it," Darlene suggested.

"I never had the slightest idea I had a twin sister," Eric said.

"And I had no idea I had a living twin brother," Darlene said.

"My parents knew there was a twin sister and they refused to take you!" Eric exclaimed. "How selfish could anyone be? To separate twins!

To take the boy but not the girl! And then to keep it a secret all these years, never telling me I had a twin sister! My parents paid to have the birth certificates altered. That is a crime!"

"Well, my parents didn't know there was a living twin brother," Darlene mused.

"Maybe we can find out more. In the meantime, you need to get an abortion as soon as possible," Eric said.

"No. I won't kill a human being. God gives life and we have no right to take it. Life begins at conception!"

"Maybe so, but all the laws allow abortion for incest," Eric said.

"Just because something is legal doesn't mean that it's right," Darlene argued. "Slavery used to be legal, too. God made our child. and He will see us through no matter what," Darlene declared.

"The child in you might have something wrong with it," Eric contended.

"That's possible. I'm going to go and talk to my minister. Do you want to go with me?" Darlene invited.

"No. I don't need some holier-than-thou guy telling me or my wife what to do. Go if you want but use your own judgment," Eric advised.

The Rev. Glen Anderson, called by his congregation, "Pastor Glen," would see Darlene that afternoon. Glen was a young man, just thirty, having graduated from a well-known theological seminary. He truly wanted to help people and made sure his office was open at all times to see anyone wanting advice. He was a short, thin man with a clean-cut appearance. He had green eyes behind thick glasses. He had a deep voice that projected easily from the pulpit every Sunday.

When Darlene knocked at the pastor's office door, her heart was beating louder than the knocking. At his "Come in," Darlene ventured to push the door open. She was breathing hard.

"What can I do for you Darlene? I'm always happy to talk to new

Christians." Pastor Glen was sitting behind a big desk cluttered with papers.

"I will come right to the point, Pastor Glen. My husband and I have a real problem."

"Oh?" the minister said. "And you have not been married yet two years, as I understand."

"That's right. Pastor Glen. We both knew we were adopted. I grew up in Denver and Eric was brought up here, not many miles from Denver. We just yesterday found out that we are twins! There was no way for anyone to know that we would meet and fall in love. But we did. The fact is that I've married my brother."

Pastor Glen was accustomed to hearing all kinds of problems, marital and otherwise. There wasn't much that could shock him. But at those words he felt is heart turn over in his chest. *"God, help me give her the right advice,"* he prayed silently.

"Well, of course you love each other, but now your love will be the love of a sister to a brother, a brother to a sister--rather than husband and wife," he said.

"We should get a divorce?" she asked.

He nodded. " Yes.Certainly, an immediate separation is on order. That doesn't mean you can't be together as friends, as siblings. You just can't, um, sleep together."

"But it isn't that simple, Pastor Glen." Now Darlene was quietly weeping. Glen handed her a tissue from the box on his desk.

"I know this is very difficult, Darlene," Glen said sympathetically.

"You don't understand it all," Darlene said, the tears gone now. She took a deep breath. "You see, the problem is complicated. I'm pregnant."

Now the pastor gripped the edge of his desk. He had thought he was shock proof. But he'd never had to deal with something like this. Why didn't they teach him how to solve a problem like this in the theological seminary?

"My husband Eric says I must have an abortion. But I don't believe in abortion for any reason, not even for rape or for incest. It is not the child's fault. God made this baby. So shouldn't I give him or her birth?"

After a pause, Pastor Glen said, "I believe you are absolutely right. We will pray about this and let God lead us."

"Eric thinks the child might not be normal." Darlene sat back in her chair.

"We can let prayer--and the Bible, God's Word--guide us. In Genesis 19 is the story of Lot's two daughters. They got their father drunk two nights in a row. The eldest daughter slept with her father the first night. The younger one slept with him the second night. The eldest daughter conceived and gave birth to a son named Moab, the father of the Moabites. The younger daughter conceived and gave birth to a son named Ben-ammi, the father of the children of Ammon or the Ammonites. Apparently, the sons that were conceived as a result of this incest had no physical defects. They grew up to have children of their own. This account of Lot's daughters tells us that people often make poor choices. They often sin. And sin does have consequences. But not every product of incest is defective. In any case, abortion is the wrong choice. You are right to reject abortion."

"That helps me," Darlene said. "So this child I carry could be normal, even though it is the product of incest?"

"Remember, all things are possible with God," the pastor said. "You have no reason to abort a child that God made and gave you. If he or she is born with a defect, God will give you the grace to deal with it. You did no wrong, as you didn't know the two of you were related. But do not sin now. Do not murder your unborn child."

"I wanted my husband Eric to talk to you, but he wouldn't come with me. He's not a Christian. I am praying for him."

"That's right," the pastor said. "And so will I. Darlene, I want you to know that I will be happy to see you or him, or both of you, at any time. Please call me any time. I'm available day and night. Let me know how you are."

Darlene nodded her agreement and rose to leave.

"Trust the Lord. It will all be OK," the pastor said.

Darlene felt better as she left, thinking of the pastor's words.

That evening when Eric came home from work, he didn't want to hear what the pastor had said. "We can go to the courthouse tomorrow and fill out some papers to get a legal divorce," he said. "I have a friend who works there. I found out that it's easy if both parties agree and no children are involved."

"Does that mean one of us has to move out of the apartment?" Darlene asked.

"We could live in the same apartment as roommates, just not as husband and wife," he reasoned. "The apartment's big enough. You can have the east half and I'll have the west half. You can have the big bedroom with the bathroom next to it. I'll take the small guest room and use the half bath next to it."

Darlene nodded her agreement. "Just until I can afford a place of my own," she said. "I know my parents would help, but I don't want to ask them."

"I understand," Eric said. "We are both adults and can take care of ourselves."

The next day Eric and Darlene completed the paperwork at the courthouse and a judge declared them divorced. Darlene was relieved that the judge did not ask them any questions about why they were divorcing. Darlene did request to take back her maiden name. So now she was no longer Darlene Carpenter. She was once again Darlene Simms.

When they got home there was a message on the answering machine. Eric's mother asked him to call her.

"I won't speak to that selfish woman," Eric said. "She and that man who calls himself my father can go—

"But Eric, they do care about you. They are the only parents you ever knew!"

"Our birth mother should have aborted us. Then neither of us would have to deal with all this!"

"Oh, Eric, please don't talk that way," Darlene pleaded. "She could have had an abortion after she was raped. But she chose to give us life. God made us and wanted us to live."

"What for? So we could be miserable all our lives?" Eric said bitterly.

"Well, at some point I suppose our parents have the right to know that we're divorced. that we're twins. It wasn't their fault that we met and fell in love."

"In a way it was their fault! If I'd known I had a twin sister--and had seen a true birth certificate--I might have wanted to check things out before I married you! But we were both in the dark. Besides, they'd just insist that you have an abortion--and you should," Eric said. "It's probably better not to tell them. It would just cause trouble."

"They'll find out we're divorced," Darlene said. "It's public information. And you know how people talk in a small town. One of the clerks at the courthouse is a friend of my mother's. She is sure to tell Mother she saw us there."

"All right. We'll tell our parents we divorced. Just not why. I'll talk to Larry and Barbara this coming weekend."

Darlene told the Simms about the divorce without giving them any details. They were sympathetic and told Darlene they would help in any way they could.

When Eric told his parents about the divorce, they were surprised. "We thought the two of you got along so well," Barbara said.

"We did!" Eric explained and left in a rage.

After that the tension between Eric and Darlene grew. Arguments became more frequent. Eric would leave. He would come back late--and drunk. They had slept in separate beds since they found out they were siblings. But Darlene could not go to sleep until she knew Eric was safe at home.

"Eric, this has to stop," Darlene said one evening when Eric came in after midnight. "I know you are driving after you've been out drinking. You could get a DWI or worse, you could have an accident and hurt yourself or someone else."

"I don' drink...don't drink.... that mush," Eric stammered.

Darlene decided it was useless to discuss the matter with him until he was sober.

CHAPTER 9

Eric and Darlene went to the adoption agency in Denver. Darlene was hoping a mistake had been made somehow.

"Larry mentioned a Mrs. Pierce. Maybe she still works there," Larry said.

When the arrived at the agency, they asked for Mrs. Pierce. A heavy woman with grey hair came to the desk. "Yes? Are you here to adopt a child?"

"No. We were both adopted through here. My father mentioned your name," Eric said.

"There was some mixed up or mistake," Darlene put in. "We recently saw our birth certificates and realized we have the same birth mother. But Eric's shows a single birth and mine shows I had a twin brother, but he died."

Darlene held out the two certificates for Mrs. Pierce to look at.

The woman suddenly turned pale. After a pause, she said, "Well, back then there were some mistakes when it came to copies of certificates. It was probably just one of those mistakes."

"Well, we've been in touch with our birth mother, and we intend to pursue this and find out who's responsible for those mistakes," Eric said.

"Excuse me but I have someone waiting to see me in the next room," Mrs. Pierce said and abruptly left.

"She's hiding something," Darlene said.

"No kidding," Eric replied. He said a few words under his breath that Darlene did not hear.

"I don't think she's going to be any help," Darlene said.

"She's not gonna come back," Eric agreed. "We're wasting our time here."

Darlene had called Jacqueline and explained what they knew about the birth certificates. Jacqueline was surprised to learn that Darlene's twin brother was alive.

Darlene had asked if she and her brother Eric could meet with her, explaining that they were in Denver. Darlene agreed, and they met in a restaurant.

"It's good to see the two of you," Jacqueline said when they had given their orders.

"Neither of us knew we had a twin," Darlene replied. "My parents didn't know there was a living twin. They were told I had a twin brother, but that he died. Eric's parents knew he was a twin but didn't tell him. We didn't know until we sent for birth certificates from the State and saw that we have the same birth mother, same date of birth."

"Someone 'doctored' the birth certificates to show that I was a single birth," Eric added. "And that Darlene's twin brother had died."

"Oh, that's incredible!" Jacqueline said. "Why would anyone do that?"

"My father, Larry Carpenter, told me he and his wife only wanted a boy and he paid to have the certificates changed. I was adopted before Darlene was adopted. The Carpenters only wanted a son, not a daughter."

"The agency knew I insisted that my twins would be adopted together!" Jacqueline exclaimed. "But then I was told the boy had died. Of course, I had no way of knowing or looking into it. I was just 16 and didn't question anything."

Darlene and Eric had decided not to tell Jacqueline that they had married and were expecting a child. It would be too much for her. It was enough of a shock for her to absorb the information they had given her.

Jacqueline was married and her two teenaged children--Jerry and Linda. They did not know about their mother's background. Jacqueline said she was going to tell them and hoped that someday Darlene and Eric could meet the two.

"We'd like that," Darlene said, and Eric agreed.

"We want to know about our birth parents. Someday if we each marry and have children, it would be good to know the genetic background," Darlene explained.

"I was raped at 16 and I was forced to choose adoption," Jacqueline said. "My maiden name was Baker."

"We are grateful that you didn't have an abortion. You could have, legally, you know," Darlene said.

"My parents wanted me to. They put a lot of pressure on me. But I refused. I also insisted that whoever adopted you would keep you two together. I didn't want you to be separated."

There was a pause. Then Jacqueline continued. "My parents were ashamed that I was pregnant out of wedlock, even if it wasn't my fault. They wanted everything kept quiet. So when I finally got married, I never told my husband, Wayne Tompson. But I'm going to tell him. It's better to be open and honest. And I know he won't blame me."

"Are you Christians?" Darlene asked.

"Yes, I am a Christian," Jacqueline said. "And my husband Wayne just recently accepted Christ," she said. "Jerry and Linda love the Lord and are active in church activities."

"I'm so glad to hear that," Darlene said.

"We don't want to bring up something unpleasant, but we were wondering about our natural father...." Eric said.

"Eric, you look so much like him that when I first saw you, I thought I'd faint! He was so handsome! He was a high school star athlete. His name was Robert Carlson. I was a cheer leader. He got me alone and, well, he forced me. I guess you want to know what he was like. Well, he was always healthy. He was a good student. He was handsome. His parents were wealthy. That's about all I know about him. I never stayed in touch, needless to say...."

"You never took him to court for what he did you?" Eric asked.

"My parents didn't want to get involved. They didn't want me to have to testify, to go through all that. So, no, we didn't file charges. They told me to just let it go. So I did. But when I found out I was pregnant--" She dropped her head into her hands.

"It must have been very hard," Eric said.

"I had a fight on my hands, as I said. They wanted to force me to abort. We fought all the time. But I won and here you are," After a pause, she said, "I plan to have a talk with Linda and Jerry to tell them about you. I know they'll want to meet you. I want to have a talk with my husband, as well."

"You have our phone numbers, so let us know and we will come and meet any time."

"That sounds like a plan," Jacqueline said.

They spent a few more minutes talking. And then after hugs and a few tears, they headed for home.

"I'm glad we didn't tell her about our marriage--or the expected baby," Darlene said. "We can explain all that to her later. Right now I think what we've told her is all she can handle."

"I agree. It's a shock to her to meet us after all these years, and to learn that there was deception involved in the adoptions."

"We'll meet with her as often as we can, and it will all work out," Darlene said.

But life was not easy after Darlene and Eric returned to their home. They continued to argue about abortion.

One evening after a fight, Eric left as usual. Darlene decided to go and find him and ask him to come home before he got drunk. There was a bar about six blocks away. Darlene decided to walk and see if Eric was there. She did not want him driving home drunk any more. She planned to persuade him to come home, and she would drive, of course.

Sure enough, their car was parked in front of the bar.

Eric was there. Darlene determined that she had to try to get him home before he got drunk and got into trouble on the way home.

Darlene approached Eric sitting at the bar, a glass in front of him.

"Eric, I'm sorry about earlier," she said, laying a hand on his shoulder. "Please come home now."

"My sister nags me more than my wife did!" Eric quipped to no one in particular.

"Please, Eric!"

"All right but I'm takin' a bottle wid me," he said, paying the bartender.

He staggered out the door with Darlene at his side.

"Git in," he said, opening the passenger side door.

"You can't drive in your condition. You're intoxicated," Darlene said. "I'll drive."

"No way," Eric yelled."No wife of mine....I mean, no sister of mine, is gonna drive me home."

Eric grabbed Darlene's arm and slammed her into the passenger seat.

"Eric! Please be reasonable!" Darlene cried.

"I'm shuch, I'm....reazon-a-bl," he said. He was behind the wheel and starting the car. Darlene was in tears. Her arm hurt from his brutal handling.

Eric began to drive--too fast.

A city dump truck was parked a couple of blocks down the street. Eric was swerving all over the road. He saw that he was too close to the curb where the truck was parked. He over corrected, lost control, then over corrected again.

"Eric!" Darlene screamed.

The car crashed straight into the dump truck.

Eric hit the horn in the center of the steering wheel with his head. The noise brought the police in short order. Eric heard the sirens and wondered what the police were doing out so late.

Darlene heard nothing.

CHAPTER 10

DARLENE OPENED HER EYES TO see her father bending over her. "Daddy?"

"Yes, Honey."

"Daddy my head hurts."

"I know, Darlene, but you're going to be fine."

"What happened?"

"Do you remember the car wreck?"

"Eric...was driving too fast."

"Yes, he hit a parked truck. It was like hitting a brick wall. He isn't hurt; and you'll be all right, thank God."

"How long have I been here...in the hospital?"

"Since last night. Oh, here's Dr. Fisher now."

"Hello, Dr. Simms. Hello, Darlene" Dr. Stanley Fisher said. "I'm glad to see you're awake now."

"Dr. Fisher?" Darlene looked at her father with a question. Dr. Fisher was an obstetrician.

"Yes. He's been taking care of you since you were brought in last night."

"You're going to be just fine, young lady," Dr. Fisher.

"My baby?"

"I'm sorry, Darlene. You lost the baby. But you can have more children," Dr. Fisher said gently.

"Oh..." Darlene was speechless. Her baby was gone. It was a shock. Then she thought maybe it is just as well, since it was a child of incest, innocent though it was. She would have had it and loved it no matter what. But now the problem was academic. She would mourn, but she had to pull herself together for Eric's sake. She and Eric were innocent victims, too—victims of deception.

"You get some rest now," Dr. Fisher suggested, turning to the door. "I'll be around again soon to check on you. I think you need some time with your father right now."

After Dr. Fisher left, Darlene's father took her hand.

"You didn't tell me you were pregnant," Dr. Simms said.

"I know, Daddy," Darlene said. "I wanted to wait until I was a little farther along."

"I understand," her father said.

There was a moment of silence. Then Darlene spoke.

"Daddy, I don't remember much at all."

"Well, that's to be expected. You suffered a concussion. You will be fine, but you must take it easy for a while. They had to give you blood, too, because you had severe blood loss."

"A blood transfusion?" Darlene was surprised.

"It saved your life. Don't worry, Honey. Now days they check the blood to be sure it's not contaminated. You won't get a disease from it. They checked your blood type and then give you the correct match from the blood bank. You have a fairly uncommon type--O Negative. But fortunately, they had enough to meet your needs."

"I read all about blood types in school," Darlene said. "And I'm not worried. I know there are four basic types, A, B, AB and 0. Everyone is either Positive or Negative."

"Yes. You're an L.P.N. You know all about these things."

"It's interesting how someone can give blood and save a life. I never realized how important blood donation is until now that my life was in danger," Darlene said.

"Yes, and now you're out of danger. Well, it's time for me to leave and let you get some sleep," Dr. Simms told his daughter.

"Daddy....where's Eric?"

"Right now he's cooling his heels in jail."

"Oh...can't you bail him out?"

Dr. Simms sighed. "We'll see. I want to know about the divorce. Why did the two of you get a divorce? Was it Eric's drinking?"

"No, Daddy. I found out he's my brother."

There was a dead silence.

Finally, Dr. Simms spoke. "Your brother?"

"We're twins. Eric was adopted just before you adopted me. The couple only wanted a baby boy. They wouldn't take me as well."

Dr. Simms fell into the chair next to Darlene's bed. There was a long silence.

"We divorced as soon as we found out we were siblings," Darlene said.

Dr. Simms was shocked. He sat a few moments with his head in his hands. Finally, Darlene's father spoke. "Your mother and I knew you had a twin brother, but we were told he had died. Do Eric's parents know that you married your twin?"

"Not yet. That's why he started drinking. We got our birth certificates and found out we had the same birth mother, and we were born on the same day. Larry Carpenter admitted to Eric that he'd had the birth certificates forged to show that Eric was a single birth and that I had a twin brother that died. They didn't want a girl, just a boy. Eric was already angry because he was what he called his being a 'replacement son.' Then he was angry that we were deceived and married. He was angry that I refused an abortion. We fought about it. He started drinking," Darlene explained.

"Anyway, after the divorce, I couldn't make Eric stop drinking. He wouldn't accept my Christian values. We argued about that. And he kept drinking more and more."

"I'll go see about bail for him," Dr. Simms sighed, got up and moved toward the door. "You're going to be OK, Honey. I'll be back later." After closing the door behind him, Dr. Simms leaned against it. His knees were weak. "Oh, God, please help us," he prayed.

Later that day Pastor Glen came into the room.

"Darlene. How are you feeling?" he asked, his voice filled with concern.

"I'm OK, thanks," she replied. She was embarrassed for her pastor to see her in a hospital bed.

"I had a talk with your father. He says you're going to be fine. I'm sorry you...lost the baby. But I thank God you're going to be all right. Your father is worried about Eric."

"I'm worried about him, too," Darlene admitted.

"Do you think he'd talk to me?"

"Maybe."

"Well, let's pray. The Lord will work things out." Glen prayed for Darlene's rapid recovery and for Eric's healing of his alcoholism. He also prayed that Eric would accept Christ and be born again.

After praying, the minister left. Darlene was glad he had come by. She felt better.

Dr. Simms put up bail for Eric to get out of jail. Eric's parents had been content to let him stay in jail. They were too angry with Eric for his drinking and driving to talk to him.

"Darlene told me about your situation," Dr. Simms told Eric, "About why you had to divorce. I think you should talk to your parents. Tell them what you found out, why you're angry. And you need to get help for your drinking problem. Darlene could have been killed—and you could have died, too. I'm sorry the unborn child did not survive, but at least Darlene is going to be make a full recovery."

"You're just full of advice, aren't you, Dr. Simms? I appreciate the bail money. I sure didn't wanna stay in that cage. And the Carpenters don't care if I rot in jail the rest of my life. But I just want Darlene to be OK. I just want everything to be all right." Eric put his hands over his eyes, as if to hide tears.

"Everything will be OK, Eric. But no more drinking! Alcohol never solved any problems."

"I'm going to go see Darlene now," Eric said.

"I should advise you about her condition first," Dr. Simms said. He gave Eric details about the concussion, the loss of the baby, and the need for a blood transfusion.

When Eric entered Darlene's room, he was feeling very guilty.

"Your dad told me what all you've been through. It's all my fault. I'm sorry, Darlene. I'll never touch another drop of liquor again," Eric vowed.

"I understand, Eric. And I'm glad you're not going to drink any more. It'll be all right."

Eric was relieved that she was going to be out of the hospital the next day. Eric took a couple of days off of work to stay with her until she felt better. Eric saw the judge and was given a suspended sentence on condition that he pay the city for the dent in the truck and get some real help for his drinking problem.

Eric began seeing a Christian counselor, Dr. Ernest Hays, twice a week. Eric stayed away from the liquor and would not even think about going into a bar again.

One evening after dinner, Eric said, "I'm sorry...about everything, Darlene."

"It's OK, Eric. I'm sorry I lost the baby."

"I'm sorry too, but now at least we won't fight about it."

"I think you should talk to your parents. Tell them about why we divorced, about the lost pregnancy, your drinking--clear the air about everything. They should know I'm your sister."

"I guess you're right. Dr. Hays says honesty is always best."

"I've asked Pastor Glen to come by tomorrow evening," Darlene announced one morning. "I think he can help us both."

"Great," was all Eric had to say.

When Pastor Glen was admitted to the apartment the next day, Darlene welcomed him with some coffee and cookies. He gladly accepted. Eric refused the refreshments. He sat in silence in a big armchair across from the sofa where the minister sat.

Darlene took another chair and began the conversation. "I invited Pastor Glen here to give us some advice on how to get on with our lives," she said.

"The best thing you can do is pray, read your Bible, and attend our Bible study classes--and church. The fellowship of other believers will be very helpful as they offer their prayers and support," the minister said, setting his coffee cup aside.

"I have to tell you, I don't believe in God; and I won't be attending any church functions," Eric said, his arms crossed at his chest. "If God exists, He isn't interested in the details of our personal lives."

"On the contrary, Eric. God knows everything about you, and He loves you more than you can imagine. Perhaps no one has ever introduced you to Jesus, the Lord and Savior. He loved you so much that He took your place, your punishment which you deserved as a sinner. He died for your sins. All you have to do is accept the free gift of salvation that He offers you; and you will belong to Him forever."

"I can't believe in a God that would let people die in a house fire, or let a child die in a swimming pool, or let six thousand Jews be annihilated," Eric said.

"God doesn't stop bad things from happening because, you see, He gave mankind free will. If someone wants to exercise free will, such as Hitler's killing Jews, God will not usually stop it. If He took free will from Hitler, He'd have to take free will from all of us. We either have free will or we don't. If we don't, then we have no choices. But with free will, we can choose God or reject Him. God doesn't want a puppet that has to do what He says because it has no choice. He wants people who worship and love Him because they want to, not because they have to. So He gave people choices: choose God or reject Him. God also does not ordinarily suspend the laws of nature. If a person chooses to jump off a building, he is going to suffer the consequences. In fact, it is a sin to tempt God, as we know when Jesus was tempted of the devil in the wilderness. The devil told Him that He should jump off a building so the angels would keep Him from getting hurt. Jesus told the devil that it is wrong to tempt God."

"So if a person kills someone, and then repents, God would forgive him. But it would not bring back the person that was murdered," Darlene put in.

"That's right. If a person commits adultery and gets a sexually transmitted disease, that person would be forgiven if he turned to God and repented. But he would still have the consequent: the disease," the preacher affirmed.

"Sin has consequences. But the sinner can be forgiven," Darlene put in.

"This is all too deep for me," Eric said.

"All you have to know to be saved is to acknowledge that you are a sinner, you can't save yourself, and repent of your sins. God sent Jesus to die in your place, God raised Him from the dead, and He is alive today," the pastor said. "Just ask Jesus to be the Lord of your life, and He will."

"So I accept Jesus and my life will be perfect?" Eric asked.

"No. Jesus said that in this world we will have tribulation. But He also said, 'Be of good cheer. I have overcome the world.' We may suffer greatly in this life. But He offers us everlasting life with Him if we put our faith and trust in Him," Glen said.

"So if I don't accept Him? I end up in hell?" Eric questioned.

"Those who reject God choose to be without God for eternity. The Bible calls that hell. Yes, it is a real place and those who go there will be there for eternity. Jesus said many would end up going there. But those who choose the straight and narrow path in following Jesus will have eternal life with Him."

"So if I'm right in my belief that there is no God or heaven or hell-- then when I die nothing happens. I just cease to exist. But if I'm wrong and there is a God-- and heaven and hell-- then when I die, I go to hell." Eric had a sarcastic smirk on his face.

"Eric, please! Pastor Glen is serious!" Darlene interjected. "Your eternal destiny depends on whether you choose Christ or reject Him, and it's no joke."

"If you are ready to accept Christ, I will pray the sinner's prayer with you and you can be saved," Pastor Glen said.

"It's just as simple as that?" Eric said.

"If you mean it in your heart when you pray it, yes," Glen replied.

"Well, OK. I need some time to think about it. Then I might let you pray that with me," Eric said.

The pastor left some gospel tracts with Eric. "These explain the plan of salvation better than I can," Glen said. "Please take time to read them. Look up the scriptures in the Bible for yourself."

Darlene saw the pastor out and turned to speak to Eric, but he had already left the room.

A few days later Eric went to see his parents. He told them about the information he and Darlene had discovered--that Darlene was the twin sister the Carpenters had rejected when they adopted Eric. He told them everything he and Darlene had been through due to the deception.

"So that's why we had to divorce," Eric explained. "Well, Dad, what have you got to say?"

Larry replied, "We meant no harm. I did pay to have the birth certificates changed. I thought it was for the best."

"You wonder why I divorced Darlene?" Eric continued. "Huh? You wonder why I got so drunk I ran into a parked truck? Well, now you know! It's your fault! How was I to know I'd married my twin—and got her pregnant!"

"We never imagined anything like that could happen," Barbara stated.

"You two are the most selfish people I know. I was never your son! I was the substitute son for your perfect Alan! I was the replacement child! Alan could do no wrong! Of course not! He was dead! You expected me to live up to the standards of a perfect child! It's no wonder I quit trying to make good grades. I didn't want to take part in any activities. I just gave up! What's the use of trying when you're competing with a 'perfect' child? I was competing with a ghost—a ghost that could do no wrong!"

Barbara was in tears.

"Why didn't you tell me?" Eric asked. "All those years you didn't tell me I had a sister! A sister that you left behind because you only wanted a son to replace the one you'd lost!"

"That's enough, Eric. I think you should leave now," Larry said firmly.

"Oh, it's enough all right. You two did enough damage to ruin my life! And Darlene's! Your fraud caused me to marry my sister! I got her pregnant! I was so upset I started drinking! I got drunk and almost killed Darlene in the car accident--and she lost the baby! I hope you're satisfied! You caused all of that by your deception when you adopted me. You two are despicable!"

"Eric, we meant no harm. We just wanted a boy. We knew someone else would adopt the girl," Barbara said. "We thought by having the birth certificates changed to show each child as a single live birth we would save the birth mother--and you, Eric--any concerns in the future."

"You thought! You just didn't want the birth mother to stop the adoption! You self-centered, evil woman!

"Take that back! Apologize to your mother!" Larry demanded.

"My mother? My real mother gave me up because she was raped and had twins?"

"You know what I mean! Apologize to Barbara!" Larry snarled.

"I won't apologize to you or to your wife. You two are not worthy to have had a child!" Eric yelled.

"I won't have you speak like that in this house!" Larry exploded.

"Oh, the house with the locked room that holds Alan's toys? The perfect of the most perfect boy? The room you kept me out of because Alan's toys were too good for me to play with?"

"Get out!" Larry demanded.

"I'm going!" Eric shouted. "There are laws against falsifying legal documents, Larry! I'm not going to forget about this!" He was white with rage as he stalked off.

CHAPTER 11

DARLENE RECOVERED AND WENT BACK to work, taking a day shift at the hospital. Eric seemed content with his job as manager at the hardware store. Darlene talked about moving into her own place, but neither she nor Eric wanted to separate, although they were now divorced and no longer involved in a romantic relationship. And, in truth, Darlene could not afford a place on just her salary. They loved each other, not as husband and wife; but there was a deep connection which they recognized as the bond between twins.

"No wonder I had nightmares as a kid," Eric told Dr. Hays at his session one afternoon. "I knew within my soul I had been separated from my sister."

"And you rebelled against your parents for what they'd done, for expecting you to be a perfect child like the one they'd lost, the one they thought of as perfect," Dr. Hays replied.

"Yes. They not only wanted me to be a perfect child. They expected me to follow in their footsteps as famous, successful people--a famous novelist and a highly respected literature professor. I wanted no part of that. So I just gave up trying," Eric admitted.

"Don't you think it's time to forgive your parents? The Lord says we must forgive those who trespass against us if we want Him to forgive us. A great healing can come out of forgiveness," Dr. Hays advised.

"Maybe. But I don't think I'm able to do that yet," Eric said.

"But you are making progress. You've stopped drinking," the counselor said.

"Yeah, I have," Eric affirmed. But he knew that was a lie. He had stopped going to bars and driving while intoxicated. He had stopped going out and coming home late. Instead, he kept bottles of Vodka hidden around the apartment and drank as often as he could get away with it.

Darlene had started seeing a man she'd met at the hospital, a physical therapist she liked. His name was Joe O'Casey. She had seen Joe at church but had not met him until they worked together. Darlene had invited him to dinner several times. He and Eric seemed to hit it off.

"I like Joe," Eric told Darlene later.

"Well, don't count on any wedding bells soon," Darlene replied. "But Joe did ask me to marry him, and I told him I'd think about it. I just didn't want to give him an answer right away. I just need time to think it over. He's a Christian man, active in the church. And I'm in love with him."

"Well, don't wait too long," Eric advised. "If he loves you, and I'm sure he must, he will be a good husband."

"Yes, you're right," Darlene agreed.

After a few moments, Eric said, "I sure wish I could find a nice girl to date."

"Why don't you ask Eleanor out?" Darlene suggested. Eleanor Chase worked at the hardware store. She seemed nice and seemed to like Eric.

"She's a lovely woman, but she's just not my type," Eric said. "She goes to church every time the door is opened. She'd expect me to become a Christian."

"That's not a bad thing, Eric," Darlene replied.

Darlene suggested that Eric find a hobby or outdoor activity to take up his time when he wasn't working. But again, Eric said he wasn't interested. So Darlene was surprised when Eric bought a 38 Special revolver and said he was going to go to the practice range once a week to shoot.

Darlene was glad that Eric was taking an interest in life again.

One evening Darlene came home from work expecting that Eric might have started dinner. He worked until five o'clock in the afternoon, but her shift didn't end until six.

When she went into the kitchen, she saw that everything was the same as it had been that morning: dishes in the sink, half a cup of cold coffee in her coffee mug, a sweater she'd left on a chair.

"Eric?" she called. "Where are you? I saw your car out front."

When there was no answer, Darlene ventured into his bedroom. There she saw Eric lying across the bed, a handgun near his hand. Her trained eyes looked for injuries and saw a wound in Eric's shoulder. There was blood on his shirt.

"Eric!" she cried.

He moaned in reply. "I was cleaning my gun. It went off."

Darlene called for an ambulance. In a few minutes, Eric was on his way to the hospital.

A doctor explained that Eric had lost some blood, but the wound to shoulder was a flesh wound and should heal with the proper care.

The next day Darlene was able to help Eric to get back to the apartment.

"I'm sorry to put you to all this trouble, Sis'," Eric said. They sat in the living room of their apartment.

"You told everyone it was an accident," Darlene said. "But I know what's going on with you. You can't fool me."

"What? What do you mean?"

"The Vodka! I thought you'd stopped drinking; but you didn't! You just hid it! Then the gun! You're depressed, Eric. You wanted to take your life; but you couldn't bring yourself to take that fatal gunshot! So when you pulled the trigger your hand jerked. You didn't really want to die."

"You're right." After a pause, Eric questioned, "You know about the Vodka?"

"You'd be surprised what I know, Eric," she said. "Remember, we're twins!"

"OK, maybe I've been depressed. You're right. I wanted to end it all. But, in fact, I don't want to die."

"Well, I hope not! Suicide is wrong! And think what it would do to me to have to live life without you!" Darlene exclaimed.

"I'm all messed up," Eric said.

"Well, that's the first step to becoming a born again Christian," Darlene said. "You must admit that you need God, that you are a sinner--and that you can't save yourself."

"I see it now," Eric said. "I need to turn to God."

Just at that moment, Pastor Glen knocked on the door.

"I came to see how you're doing," he said as he entered. "I've been praying for you, Eric."

"Eric is ready to accept Christ," Darlene said. "Please join us here in the living room and help me explain the scriptures to Eric."

After the exchange of a few pleasantries, Glen said, "So, Eric, are you ready to accept the Lord as your Savior?"

"Yes. I want what Darlene has, what you have. I want the Lord in my life, " Eric said.

"Salvation is a free gift," Glen replied. "The Bible says, 'For all have sinned, and come short of the glory of God.' That's Romans 3:23. God cannot tolerate sin. Romans 6:23 says, 'For the wages of sin is death; but the gift of God is eternal life through Jesus Christ our Lord.' And in Ephesians 2:8 and 9, it says, 'For by grace are ye saved through faith; and that not of yourselves: it is the gift of God: Not of works, lest any man should boast.'" You can't save yourself by good works. Salvation is God's gift. It's His grace that saves you."

"OK. I'm a sinner and I can't save myself," Eric admitted.

"The soul that sins is condemned to die. But Jesus took our sins--yours and mine--on Himself and died for us, in our place," the pastor explained. "Isaiah 53:6 says, 'All we like sheep have gone astray; we have turned everyone to his own way; and the Lord hath laid on him the iniquity of us all.' From the beginning of the world, God had a plan to redeem mankind after the sin of the first people when they disobeyed God. Satan tempted them and they fell. But God had a plan, as revealed in Genesis 3:15: 'And I will put enmity between thee and the woman, and between thy seed and her seed; it shall bruise thy head, and thou shalt bruise his heel.' God was speaking to Satan, telling him that there would be a Redeemer who would defeat him, even though it be at the great cost of death on the cross. God's plan was carried out through the virgin birth, Christ's sinless life, and His taking our sins upon Himself. When Christ arose from the grave, He had conquered sin, death and the grave. In His glorified body He was seen of many people before He ascended to heaven, leaving His disciples to watch for His return, even while carrying out the Great Commission to take the gospel to the world."

"OK," Eric said. "I guess I see that."

Then Darlene spoke up. "Look. What if you were guilty of a terrible crime, like murder, and the judge condemned you to the death penalty. You admitted you deserved it. But then your lawyer stepped up and said, 'Execute me instead of him. Let me take his place.' And the judge says, 'Well, someone has to pay; and if you want to be the substitute for this man, then you can die in his place.' The thing is, the substitute--the sacrifice, if you will, had to be perfect. Jesus could not have died for us if He had been a sinner Himself. But He never sinned. So God allowed Him to die for us," Darlene explained.

"That's right," Glen added. "Jesus is the only Man who never sinned, so He was able to be the sacrifice for our sins--the Lamb of God."

Eric picked up one of the tracts Pastor Glen had left. "I've been meaning to read this," he said.

"Good," Pastor Glen said. He opened the tract and pointed to a verse inside. "John 3:16 says, 'For God so loved the world, that he gave his only begotten Son, that whosoever believeth in him should not perish, but have everlasting life.'"

"That's what you need to know and accept, Eric," Darlene said. "You are so much loved! God loved you from the time He made you! Jesus loved you enough to suffer and die for you. He died in your place. And if you accept Him as your Savior, He will give you everlasting life."

"So the way to God is to accept Jesus as the Lord of my life?" Eric asked. "There is no other way?"

Glen replied, "In John 14:6 Jesus said, 'I am the way, the truth, and the life: no man cometh unto the Father, but by me.' And in Acts 4:12, it says, 'Neither is there salvation in any other; for there is no other name under heaven given among men, whereby we must be saved.' Jesus said He is standing at the door of your heart, He said, 'Behold, I stand at the door, and knock: if any man hear my voice, and open the door, I will come in to him, and will sup with him, and he with me.'-- Revelation 3:20."

"What if He turns me away?" Eric said.

"That won't happen," Glen said. "Jesus never turns anyone away who comes to Him sincerely. In Revelation 22:17, it says, 'And let him that is athirst come. And whosoever will, let him take of water of life freely.' And in John 6:37 Jesus said, '...him that cometh to me I will in no wise cast out.'"

Looking at the tract, Eric read: "'Verily, verily, I say unto you, He that heareth my word, and believeth on him that sent me, hath everlasting life, and shall not come into condemnation; but is passed from death unto life.'--John 5:24."

"That's just what Jesus said. Those are His words. And He is speaking to you, Eric, just as He speaks to anyone wanting to be saved," Darlene said. "God loves you, Eric."

"Are you ready to commit your life to Christ?" Glen asked. "Are you ready to be born again?"

"Yes," Eric said softly. "I know that Jesus was my substitute at the cross. He died in my place, for my sins."

"Then we'll say the sinner's prayer with you," Pastor said. "Darlene and I will pray with you. If you say these words and believe them in your heart, you will be saved." After a pause he prayed, "Heavenly Father, I know that I'm a sinner. I know I can't save myself. I believe Jesus, the Son of God, died on the cross for me. He took my sins upon Himself. I repent of my sins. I turn from my sins. I receive you, Jesus, as my Lord and Savior. I believe You died in my place and then rose from the dead and are alive forevermore. Please forgive my sins, come into my life and save me. Thank you for what You did on the cross for me. Father, I pray this prayer in the name of Jesus. Amen."

After Eric had prayed the prayer led by Glen, there was silence. Finally, Eric asked, "So Jesus is in heaven with God? Yet He can be with me, in my heart?"

"Yes, the Holy Spirit has come into your heart. After Jesus was raised from the dead and spent some time on earth with His disciples and was seen of many, He ascended into heaven, as we read in the book of Acts. He is at the right hand of the Father. But the Holy Spirit was sent to be with all believers. He comes into your heart the moment you are saved, and He will never leave you. Now that you have accepted Christ, He dwells in your heart. The mystery of the trinity is difficult to understand. But the Father, the Son, and the Holy Ghost provide all we need."

"And Jesus will return to earth again, as He promised," Darlene put it. "And it may be soon! We want to be ready."

"When I prayed that prayer, I felt a sense of peace come over me that I've never felt before," Eric observed.

"That's the Holy Spirit. He will be with you always," Glen explained.

"I know I've been born again," Eric said. "I want to be baptized."

"Yes, that is right," Glen said. "We can arrange that. And when you attend church, you should come forward to let the congregation know that you've accepted Christ and that you want to follow Him in baptism. Romans 10: 9-10 says, 'That if thou shalt confess with thy mouth the Lord Jesus, and shalt believe in thine heart that God hath raised him from the dead, thou shalt be saved. For with the heart man believeth unto righteousness, and with the mouth confession is made unto salvation.' Jesus said, 'Whosoever, therefore, shall confess me before men, him will I confess also before my Father, who is in heaven. But whosoever shall deny me before men, him will I also deny before my Father, who is in heaven.' You'll find that in Matthew 10:32-33. As far as baptism, Acts 2:38 says, '...Repent and be baptized every one of you in the name of Jesus Christ for the remission of sins, and ye shall receive the gift of the Holy Ghost.'"

"Yes! I'm ready to be baptized," Eric said.

"Then I'll go and make the arrangements now," Glen said, rising.

"Pastor Glen, I have resented my parents all my life. But now I have it in my heart to forgive them. I do forgive them. I want them to know. And I want them to become Christians as well."

"That is good. I would be glad to visit them at any time and help them understand how to be saved," Glen said.

"I'll talk to them first and then let's meet with them, if they are willing," Eric said.

"That sounds good, Eric. And I'm glad you have forgiven them. Jesus wants us to forgive everyone, just as the Father forgives us," Glen said.

"I realized that when I accepted Him."

The three of them spent a few more minutes talking and then Glen excused himself.

"Thank you for your help, Pastor Glen," Darlene said.

"The angels in heaven are rejoicing as they always do when a soul is saved," Glen said. "We have good reason to be joyful and glad this evening."

CHAPTER 12

ERIC HAD NEVER FELT SO much peace in his life. He wasn't angry most of the time as he had been. He found it in his heart to forgive everyone in his life who had caused him pain, especially Barbara and Larry. He made a point of seeing them and apologized for his previous behavior.

"I'm a Christian now and I have been forgiven of my sins. I forgive you for hurting me and I ask you to forgive me for hurting you."

"Well, you're our son. Of course, we forgive you," Barbara said. Larry nodded in agreement.

"Maybe the two of you will go to church with me or maybe go to a Bible study class," Eric suggested.

"We've never been churchgoers, but we aren't bad people," Barbara said. "We don't believe in organized religion."

"Well, Jesus wasn't fond of the organized religion of His day, either. But God wants a personal relationship with you. That's what's important. You're not 'bad people,' as you said. But everyone has sinned. 'For all have sinned and come short of the glory of God,' it says in Romans 3:23. Everyone needs Christ."

"We'll think about it," Barbara promised.

"Would it be all right if our paster, Glen Anderson, came with me to visit with you sometime?"

"Maybe," Larry said. "But he's not going to convince me to believe in God and become a Christian."

"We just don't want someone pushing religion down our throats," Barbara explained.

"Oh, of course not," Eric said. "God gave everyone free will. It's your choice."

"Yeah. I don't need a crutch to get me through life," Larry said. "And that's what religion is--a crutch."

"Religion can't save you. The church can't save you. Jesus just wants a relationship with you as your Savior. It's good to find a church where you can worship with other believers, of course; but your salvation comes from faith in Christ and what He did at the cross."

"Eric, you're starting to sound like a religious fanatic," Barbara said.

"I don't know about names or labels," Eric replied. "I just know Jesus. And I know He loves you. He died for your sins. And He wants you to accept the free gift of salvation. He wants to be your Lord and Savior."

"We'll think it over," Barbara said, moving to the door. "You come back any time, Eric. And if you want to bring the pastor, I think that would be fine."

"Yeah. Later, Son. Later," Larry said, rising and moving toward the door as well.

They obviously wanted Eric to leave. All this talk about Jesus was making them uncomfortable.

Later, Eric spoke to Darlene about his visit.

"They couldn't get me out of there fast enough," Eric said. "The Holy Spirit was convicting their hearts of their sins. That is what He does to try to get people to turn to Christ.

Barbara believes in God, I think, but she doesn't have a relationship with Jesus. As for Larry, he has never believed in God and claims to be an atheist."

"Well, maybe if Barbara accepts Christ as her Savior, then Larry may be converted."

"I hope so," Eric said. "I want them to know how much God loves them. I want them to know the joy of salvation."

CHAPTER 13

Darlene continued to see Joe O'Casey and had told him she would marry him. Joe had been a Christian for several years and attended church with Darlene. Joe's parents were no longer living, and he had been an only child. He was lonesome and loved Darlene. It seemed that they made a perfect couple. But Darlene needed a little time.

Eric thought there should be a big wedding. "Go all out," he told Darlene.

"I'd like that," Darlene said. "My parents would insist on paying for it, but we could help."

"Sure, we could," Eric agreed. "And if we start planning now, it can all come together next year."

"Well, Joe is all for it," Darlene said. "I'd like to tell our birth mother about Joe. And we could tell her, you know, about us, what we've been though, and how the Lord has helped us."

Darlene called Jacqueline Baker and asked if they could meet.

The next week Eric and Darlene met Jacqueline in a small cafe in a town just outside of Denver. Jacqueline seemed genuinely glad to see them again. They told Jacqueline about their meeting, getting married, expecting a baby, the wreck, and the miscarriage—all due to Larry's fraud in having the birth certificates changed with Nancy Pierce's culpability.

"I don't know what to say," Jacqueline said. "You've been through so much!"

"We can't change the past," Darlene said. "But our future is in God's hands. We are trusting the Lord to lead us."

"Yes, you're right. I'm just sorry you two had to go through all that," Jacqueline said.

"Life isn't fair and people are often unkind. If we can forgive those who wrong us and move on with our lives, that's a good thing," Jacqueline continued. "My parents never understood why I didn't want to have an abortion after I'd been raped. I'd have kept you if I could have, but my parents would not have supported us. And I had no way to support myself at age 16. I tried my best to think of a way I could keep you. Even though Robert Carlson had raped me, I hoped that somehow he'd make it right. I called him on the phone and told him I was pregnant from what he'd done to me. I hoped and prayed he would apologize for what he'd done. I prayed he'd tell me that he loved me, would marry me, and we would have a future together. Then I could have kept you and you'd have had your own mother and father. I would have forgiven him, and things would be wonderful. I was dreaming, of course, living in a fantasy world. But I think his parents would have helped us if we had asked. The Carlsons had plenty of money. They spoiled Robert and gave him whatever he wanted. So I thought maybe he'd want to marry me. But Robert just laughed at me and told me I'd been with so many boys I couldn't know who the father was. He said if I accused him, he'd get his football buddies to testify that they'd had sex with me, too, and that no one could prove he was the father of my baby. There was no DNA testing. I was really hurt; he broke my heart. I'd never been with another boy before Robert, but he made me feel like a....like--"

"It's OK. We understand," Eric broke in.

"We didn't know if we should tell you all this, but we thought about it a lot. We just want you to know we are grateful to you. You did the right thing and brought us into the world. It isn't your fault that some selfish people caused us problems," Darlene said." We just wanted to be honest and open with you. We know you and your husband are Christians. We recently accepted Christ and are letting all our friends and family know."

"I'm glad. I rejoice with you." Jacqueline said. "You went through a lot, but the Lord will direct your path, just as He directed mine when Robert ran out on me."

"We've realized the importance of forgiving those who have hurt us," Darlene said. "We know the scriptures tell us that is what our Lord wants. Matthew 6:14 and 15 says, "'For if ye forgive men their trespasses, your heavenly Father will also forgive you: But if ye forgive not men their trespasses, neither will your Father forgive your trespasses.'"

"Yes, and we pray in the Lord's Prayer, as given in Matthew 6: 'Forgive us our trespasses, as we forgive them that trespass against us.'"

"With the grace of God, we are able to forgive," Eric said. "The Holy Spirit within us gives us that ability."

"Yes, in Matthew 18, Jesus gave the parable of the unforgiving servant," Jacqueline said. "The man owed a lot of money and begged his lord to forgive his debt—which he did. But then that same servant went to a fellow servant who owed him money and did not forgive his debt. So the master called that servant and asked, 'Shouldest not thou also have had compassion on thy fellow servant, even as I had pity on thee?' And the unforgiving servant was punished, Jesus said that the heavenly Father would do the same to an unforgiving person."

"I'm glad we're able to forgive," Eric said.

They needed to get home, so Eric and Darlene promised Jacqueline to meet with her again soon.

After they left, Darlene said, "I'm glad we met with Jacqueline and told her the truth."

"The truth is always best," Eric agreed.

"That poor girl went through a terrible ordeal, and yet she fought for us to have life," Darlene said. "But now she has a good life. She's a kind, Christian woman with a good family. I'm glad she's our mother. Of course, we love the parents who brought us up. But our birth mother is very special."

Eric nodded in agreement.

CHAPTER 14

FOR SEVERAL WEEKS LIFE WAS routine, but it was good. Eric went to work at the hardware store. Darlene worked at the hospital. Joe liked his job at the hospital as a physical therapist. He and Darlene were making wedding plans. Darlene's parents started attending church with them and soon committed their lives to Christ.

"We knew about the Christian faith, in a way," Judy said. "Bill and I attended a church once in a while--on Christmas or Easter. And of course, we'd been in church for weddings and funerals. But we'd never learned how to know Jesus, to really know Him as our Personal Lord and Savior. When we attended church with Darlene, the pastor explained the plan of salvation and we realized we were lost without Christ."

"That's right," Bill said. "I studied science all my life. As a medical doctor, I thought science had all the answers. When I started reading the Bible, I realized that God is in control of everything. We humans can only do what He allows us to do, and He wants a relationship with us more than anything. God sent Jesus to redeem us, to reconcile us to Himself, so we might spend eternity in His presence. God became man in order to save 'whosoever will.' Anyone can come to Christ and receive the hope of eternal life in Him."

"We're all going to live forever," Judy agreed. "But only believers in Christ will live with Him in heaven. Those who reject Christ will spend eternity in hell. A lot of preachers these days don't want to preach about hell. They want people to just feel good. But Jesus taught about hell and said that many will go there because they reject Him."

Eric's hoped his parents would soon accept Christ and be baptized in obedience to Christ. They were getting ready to leave on a trip to France, so Eric asked if he and Pastor Glen could visit with them before they left. Reluctantly, Barbara agreed.

Eric and Glen went to the Carpenter home after dinner one evening. Pastor Glen brought his Bible and an extra Bible along. They sat in the living room to talk.

"I know you probably have a Bible," Glen told the couple. "But I'd like to give you this one as a gift. It's a special study Bible and may answer many of your questions."

"I don't see how," Larry replied. "The Bible was written by men and has been translated many times. It can't be accurate, and it is full of contradictions."

"If you study the whole Bible, you'll see that it makes sense. It was inspired by the Holy Spirit as He gave men the inspiration to write. II Timothy 3:15 says, 'All scripture is given by inspiration of God, and is profitable for doctrine, for reproof, for correction, for instruction in righteousness.'"

"So the Bible says the Bible is true. That's pretty weak," Larry countered.

"We know you preachers always say to take things by faith, but we demand proof," Barbara said.

"God never attempts to prove himself," Glen said. "The book of Genesis does not try to convince us that God exists. It assumes that God exists and that we know it. Yes, we have to take things by faith," Glen replied. "But a study of God's Word will convince you that it is the inspired, infallible Word of God. And, yes, the Bible says we need to have faith."

"Well, we don't believe in those Christian miracles like the virgin birth and the resurrection of Christ," Barbara said.

"Such things are myths. Those things couldn't really happen," Larry agreed.

"You mean the God who created the universe, including humans, wouldn't be able to do those things?" Eric put in.

"I believe in the big bang and the theory of evolution," Larry said. "The earth is millions of years old."

"Well, that's just a theory and no one can prove it. But I'm not here to argue with you. I just want you to know that God loves you and wants a relationship with you. You can have that if you accept Jesus as your Lord and Savior. Sin separated man from God, but Jesus is the way God provided to reconcile mankind to Himself," Glen said.

"I didn't know the truth of the Gospel, but I listened to Pastor Glen and others--and I accepted Christ. I wish you would consider doing the same," Eric urged. "I prayed what is known as 'The Sinner's Prayer.' You simply tell God that you are sorry for your sins and that you want to follow Christ, commit your life to Him."

"Well, it's nice of the two of you to be concerned, but we have our own way of thinking and I doubt we are going to change," Larry said, rising from his place on the sofa.

"Maybe another time we can discuss this more," Barbara said. "After we get back from our trip to France. We're leaving in a couple of days and plan to stay a few months."

So Eric and Glen left, both feeling disappointed that the Carpenters had not been open to accepting Christ into their lives.

CHAPTER 15

One day Darlene had a phone call from Eleanor Chase, the young woman who worked at the hardware store with Eric. She said she was worried about Eric. He had started dropping things, losing things, forgetting things. Sometimes he'd stare off into space and wouldn't hear anyone talking to him for a few moments. Sometimes he stumbled and almost fell. Eleanor had asked him once when he almost fell if he was OK. He had replied that he sometimes had "dizzy spells."

"Eric said he'd been having headaches and sometimes loses his balance. He also mentioned that he thinks he needs glasses. I know Eric used to have a drinking problem, but he doesn't anymore, does he?" she asked.

"No. Eric hasn't touched a drop of liquor since he committed his life to Christ," Darlene replied.

"Well, you're a nurse, so I thought you should know that maybe Eric needs a checkup or something," Eleanor said.

"Well, the first thing I'm going to do is check his blood pressure," Darlene said. "And then I'll make sure he goes in for a thorough health check-up. Thank you for telling me what you've noticed."

"Thanks, Darlene. I don't want to seem like a busy-body or something. I was just concerned," Eleanor said.

"I understand, and I appreciate your concern," Darlene said.

With two women insisting that he see a doctor, Eric didn't have much choice. Besides, he sensed that something was not right.

Eric saw his family doctor and then he was referred to a neurologist, Dr. Brice Parker. He had several tests done. Finally, when he had the test results, he called Eric into his consultation room. Dr. Parker was known as a brilliant man, but he did not have a particularly good "bedside manner." He got right to the point.

"The tests show that you have a brain tumor," he said without preface.

"What?"

"It's inoperable," the doctor continued.

"So there's nothing to do?" Eric questioned.

"We could try radiation and some experimental types of chemotherapy. But results from past patients with your type of growth have not been encouraging," the doctor said.

"In other words, those things would be expensive, maybe painful, and still would not be a cure," Eric surmised.

"That's about right," Dr. Parker agreed. "But it's up to you."

"How long can I keep working?"

"You shouldn't be working now," the doctor answered.

"I...I don't know what to say," Eric mumbled.

"There's only so much we can do, and we can't guarantee good results. I can provide you with some medications that will make you more comfortable, especially as time progresses."

"Well, how much time do I...do I have left?" Eric asked.

"I would say six months to a year," the doctor said. "But of course, no one can say for sure."

"If it was you, Doctor, what would you do?"

"I'd go home and enjoy life as long as I could. You'll eventually need a caregiver. This isn't something you can do alone. Of course, there are some good home health care agencies that can step in to help when you get to that point--and finally, hospice care."

Eric left the office in a fog. He thought of the scene from the 1970 movie, "Love Story." He'd seen it on a TV channel that showed old movies. He remembered the scene where the young husband, Oliver, played by Ryan O'Neal, learns that is wife is dying of cancer. The wife, Jenny, played by Ali McGraw, had not yet been told by her doctor, but Oliver had just spoken with the man and had been told that his wife was going to die. As Oliver left the doctor's office, the dissonant music as he walked along the street filled his brain. It was as though he could see nothing, hear nothing, only the discordant music. He was in shock. He couldn't think. That's just how Eric felt as he left the doctor's office. He was going to die--soon.

That evening Darlene suggested they go out to see a movie.

"I don't want to see a movie," Eric said. "I just want to talk."

"I can see something's bothering you, Eric. What is it?"

"I saw Dr. Parker today. He has the results of the tests. I have an inoperable tumor in the brain."

Darlene was stunned.

"Maybe it's a mistake," she finally managed.

"It's no mistake. You know I've been having those headaches lately," he replied.

"I'm calling Pastor Glen," Darlene said.

Glen came over to their place right away. He tried to encourage them. "Eric, a doctor's diagnosis isn't necessarily a death sentence," he said. "Life and death are in God's hands. Only He decides when your life is this world is over."

"I know. I'm just afraid I'm going to die soon," Eric said.

"None of us has been guaranteed another day. We don't know what minute the Lord will call us home. But if we are ready, we can say with Paul in Roman 14, 'For whether we live, we live unto the Lord; and whether we die, we die unto the Lord; whether we live therefore, or die, we are the Lords.' That verse 8 is very encouraging."

"Yes, it is," Eric agreed.

"Paul was persecuted and endangered throughout his preaching career. He suffered all kinds of abuse. He never knew when his life might be taken. But he was ready," Glen said. "He wrote in 2 Corinthians 5:8: 'We are confident, I say, and willing rather to be absent from the body, and to be present with the Lord. Wherefore we labor, that, whether present or absent we may be accepted of him.'"

"What should we do, Pastor?" Darlene asked. "We know when we die, we will go to be with the Lord. But Eric may be facing a serious.... possibly a fatal...illness. How can we deal with that?"

"James 5:14 and 15 says, 'Is any sick among you? let him call for the elders of the church; and let them pray over him, anointing him with oil in the name of the Lord: And the prayer of faith shall save the sick.....' I am going to call together some of the people from the church; and we will meet and pray for Eric. God is the same today as he was in the time of Christ. Jesus has not changed. He can heal you, Eric. I will call tomorrow and let you know when we can all meet. Let's believe the Lord together," Glen said.

After praying with Eric and Darlene, the minister left. Darlene and Eric talked quietly.

"The doctor said if this progresses, as he expects, I'll need a caregiver," Eric said.

"That would be me," Darlene replied. "I'm a nurse and I'm your sister. You can be sure I will always be with you to help you."

"I know you will," Eric said. "But I believe God is going to heal me."

"No matter how long or how short our lives, we know that we have eternal life with Jesus Christ, our Lord, to whom we have committed ourselves," Darlene said.

"I'm glad I accepted Christ as my Savior. You led me to Him. I'll always be grateful to you for that," Eric told her. "And that we found each other."

CHAPTER 16

"I NEED TO CALL LARRY AND Barbara," Eric said. I don't want them to be upset. I certainly don't want them to cut their trip to France short. I just think it's only fair for them to know. If they found out later, they'd be upset that I didn't call and tell them."

"You're right, Eric," Darlene said.

Larry answered the telephone at his hotel room that evening.

"Oh, Eric. I'm glad you called," Larry said. "We attended a wonderful concert. I know your mother will want to tell you all about it."

"Dad, I'm calling to tell you I had tests done at the hospital. Dr. Parker met with me and told me I have a brain tumor. I might only have six months to live. I don't want you and mom to change your plans. I'm trusting the Lord to heal me. But I just wanted you to know. It wouldn't be right not to tell you."

There was silence on the other end of the line as Larry digested what Eric had told him.

"You should get a second opinion, and then a third. Tests can be wrong, you know," Larry said.

"I'm getting a second opinion this week, Dad," Eric said. "Whatever happens, I've decided I'm going to go to Bible college and go into full time work for the Lord, maybe become a minister—if the Lord gives me the time."

"What?" Larry exploded." That's utterly ridiculous! That tumor must have affected your reasoning power!"

"Dad, with the time I have left, six months or sixty years, whatever it is, I want to serve the Lord. He loved me enough to die for my sins. I want to live for Him. If I can't become a minister, I'll serve Him as I can each day. If He heals me, then I'll go to Bible college."

"Now I know you're not thinking right," Larry said. "Mom and I will be starting home as soon as we can. I've got to know all the facts about this so-called brain tumor. I don't think the doctors can be right. In any case, I want to have a talk with you about this nonsense of serving God."

Eric talked briefly to Barbara. "I don't want you to cut your trip short. Tell Dad I'm OK. Nothing is going to happen in the next few weeks, anyway."

Barbara was holding back tears, but she said, "All right, Eric. We'll see." But she knew they would be returning home as soon as they could.

Pastor Glen and three other men, including Darlene's fiancé, Joe, came to visit Eric and Darlene the next evening. They anointed Eric with oil and prayed for his healing. Eric felt sure the Lord was healing him. But he was prepared for anything, knowing he was in God's hands.

Eric made a list of some things he wanted to do--whether or not the Lord healed him.

"I want us to meet with Jacqueline and our half-brother and half-sister," Eric told Darlene the next morning. "Can we make the trip next week?"

"Yes. I'll call Jacqueline and see if that will work for her," Darlene said.

"I'm trusting the Lord for healing," Eric said. "But, in any case, I want to do some things that are important. I want to spend some time with Jacqueline—and the Linda and Jerry.

"We should always do the things that are important. We never know what day will be our last," Darlene said. "None of us know when the Lord will call us home."

The meeting was set up, so Eric and Darlene made the trip to meet Jacqueline and her two children, Jerry and Linda. Darlene drove the car while Eric relaxed and enjoyed the scenery along the way.

"I think Colorado must have some of the most beautiful mountains in the world," Eric said. "Not that I've traveled to see all the others!"

"Well, it certainly is a beautiful state," Darlene agreed. "And if the Lord wills, someday you may have an opportunity to travel and see all kinds of mountains."

"Yes, if we have the time. Darlene, we know the Lord Jesus promised to return. When He ascended into heaven, the angels told his disciples that He would return in the same manner as He was taken up. I read it in the first chapter of the book of Acts."

"Yes. The Lord could return at any time," Darlene agreed. "And when he does, He will make everything right."

"We must all be ready. We must watch and pray and be ready to receive our King of Kings," Eric said.

"We are told in the Bible to watch because we know not when our Lord will appear," Darlene agreed. "No one knows the day or hour when He will appear. But we need to be ready."

"Yes," Eric agreed.

They met in a park and had a picnic lunch that Jacqueline had prepared. It was a good meeting. Linda and Jerry were very friendly teenagers and were interested in knowing Eric and Darlene better.

"I want you to meet my husband, Wayne," Jacqueline said. "But he works so much it's hard for him to get away. He's the owner of a plumbing company."

"Well, maybe if he can get some time off, we can arrange to come and meet him whenever it's convenient for him. We'd sure like to meet him," Darlene said.

"That's good. I'll keep in touch and let you know," Jacqueline agreed.

Eric explained his health condition. He explained that the church had been praying for him and he was trusting God for healing.

Jacqueline seemed concerned but cheerful. "I believe the Lord will heal you, Eric," she said. She was putting the remains of the meal back into her picnic basket.

"Well, it's entirely up to Him. I want His will to be done in my life, and I am hoping He will give me more years in the future. I'd like to go to a Bible college and then have some kind of full-time ministry work, maybe even be a missionary," Eric explained.

"If that's what you want, then you should go for it," Jacqueline said.

"Well, I'd have to be healthy to do all that, so I need the Lord to heal me," Eric said. "My headaches and dizzy spells have not leveled off any. But I'm trusting that they will."

"Sometimes God heals instantly. Other times he heals gradually. Sometimes He heals through medicine. He can use people such as doctors and nurses to help us. Whatever His will is, He will never leave us or forsake us," Jacqueline said.

"We're so grateful we got to meet with you and Linda and Jerry," Darlene said. "This has been a wonderful visit."

"Well, let's not leave the park until we pray for Eric," Jacqueline said. Linda, Jerry, and Darlene gathered around Eric. Jacqueline led the prayer, asking for a total healing of Eric's body. She rebuked the tumor in Eric's brain and commanded it to leave in the name of Jesus.

"I believe the Lord is healing you," Jacqueline said.

"We believe, as well," Darlene affirmed.

Then they all said good-bye "until we meet again."

CHAPTER 17

Barbara and Larry were back in the States four days later. Leaving the plane in Denver, they rented a car to travel back to their hometown.

It was late afternoon by the time they started out, traveling west of Denver, heading toward the small town west and south of the big city.

"You're tired, Larry. Maybe we should get a motel and drive on home tomorrow."

"It's not that far to drive on home!" Larry asserted.

"I know. But you don't like driving in the dark," Barbara declared.

"I won't have to drive in the dark very long," Larry countered.

"Well, neither of us is as young as we used to be," Barbara said.

"Oh, stop nagging me," Larry snapped. He was angry and stepped on the accelerator. They were on a two-lane highway with a high ridge on one side and a deep drop off into a canyon on the other.

It had started to rain, a first with a soft shower. But then the rain came heavily, and the highway had a couple of inches of water on it. Larry did not slow down in spite of the rain. Larry started to pass a truck when the headlights of an oncoming vehicle warned him to get back into his lane. Larry swerved, over corrected, and suddenly the car hydroplaned on the wet pavement and crashed through the guard rail. The car came to a rest before plunging down into the canyon, but it was facing downhill in a precarious position. Only the guard rail and a few boulders had kept it from plunging into the canyon.

At the same time, Dr. Roger Mason was traveling home from a medical convention in Denver. This was his first trip to Colorado. He had a thriving practice in New Mexico--a nice home and a loving family--wife Sharon and his boys, Billy and Johnny.

Suddenly Dr. Mason saw a car ahead of him veer off the road and crash through the guard rail. He pulled over to the side of the road near the crashed vehicle. After calling for help on his cell phone, the doctor took a flashlight and carefully found his way to the site of the wreck.

The man was unconscious, but his vital signs were stable. The woman, however, was bleeding profusely. Dr. Mason could stop the bleeding from the woman's head; but he feared she was bleeding internally. Her vital signs were not good. She was moaning.

"I'm a doctor--Dr. Roger Mason. Help is on the way," Roger said aloud. "Hang on."

"I don't think I'm going to make it," the woman said, struggling to get each word out.

"Help is coming. You'll be at the hospital soon," Dr. Mason said in an encouraging voice. "What is your name?"

"Barbara Carpenter. My husband...Larry. How is he?"

"He's all right for the moment. I think he'll be fine. Don't worry," the doctor replied. "Trust the Lord."

"Are you a Christian?" Barbara asked.

"Yes, I am," Roger affirmed.

"Pray with me," the woman managed to say.

Roger Mason replied. "I'll pray with you."

The woman uttered the "sinner's payer" that Eric told her about. "God, I'm sorry for my sins. . . .Forgive my sins. I know Christ took my sins to the cross and paid the price for them. I accept Jesus as my Savior...."

Roger prayed it with her.

"Doctor, I believe the Lord has saved me," the woman said.

"Yes, He has," Dr. Mason assured her. "And now you can live for Christ for the rest of your life."

"And be with Him forever...." her voice trailed off.

"Yes," Roger agreed. The doctor checked the woman's vital signs. He knew she was bleeding inside and there was nothing he could do about it. He held her hand until the ambulance came. By that time the hand was growing cold.

CHAPTER 18

Dr. Roger Mason stayed at the scene of the wrecked car until the police arrived. He had done what he could to make Larry comfortable, but the unconscious man, undoubtedly suffering from a concussion, did not respond to the doctor's voice.

The doctor gave a statement to the police and told the Emergency Medical Technicians all he could about the injuries Barbara and Larry had sustained.

"Barbara and Larry Carpenter," the doctor said. "That's what the woman told me their names were. I wasn't able to get any information--where they live, where they were going...."

"That's all right, Doctor. You probably saved the man's life. That's a deep scalp wound, and you stopped the bleeding," one of the EMT's said. "Looks like a compound fracture of the femur. Denver's the nearest hospital, so we're headed back that way."

"I'm sorry I couldn't help his wife," Roger said. "I believe she succumbed to internal injuries."

"It looks like you did all you could," one of the police officers declared.

"Well, I prayed with her. I'm afraid that's all I could do."

"Maybe that's the most important thing," the officer added.

"We're ready to roll," an E.M.T. said.

Roger called Sharon on his cell phone to tell his wife he'd be a little late.

When Roger finally arrived home, Sharon met him at the door. "Roger, I've been worried," Sharon said as her husband embraced her. "Tell me what happened."

"Oh, Sharon. I'm wiped out. There was a car wreck." The doctor sat his medical bag on the floor by the sofa and took off his coat.

"Oh, Roger, there's blood all over your coat!"

"I don't doubt it," Roger replied. "The man will probably live. He didn't regain consciousness while I was there, but if he gets good care at the hospital, he may be all right. But the woman died in my arms."

"Oh, Roger, Darling--"

"She had internal injuries. I couldn't help her. But she asked me to pray with her, and I did. She accepted Christ as her Savior."

"Oh, Roger, you led a soul to Christ!"

"She was ready. She wanted to pray. All I did was pray with her. Now she is with Jesus."

"And the husband may not be a Christian," Sharon said.

"I don't know. I'm going to make a trip to Denver day after tomorrow; and I'll check with the hospital to see how Larry Carpenter is doing. In any case, I would like to contact him and tell him that his wife accepted Christ before she died."

"Yes, Roger. That would be good," Sharon said. "You did a good thing tonight."

"Only because the Lord directs my path," Roger said. "Let's turn in."

"And thank God for His help," Sharon said.

Roger nodded his agreement.

CHAPTER 19

It was nearly five o'clock in the morning when Eric awoke to pounding on the door.

He wondered who in his right mind would be knocking on the door at this hour.

"I'm coming," he shouted, hoping he didn't wake Darlene in the other bedroom.

Eric was surprised to see a Colorado State Trooper in his grey uniform standing at the door. Another trooper was walking up behind the first one, apparently a partner.

"What?" Eric said more to himself than to the men as he opened the door.

"We're looking for Eric Carpenter," the trooper at the door said.

"I'm Eric."

"I'm Officer Alex Mayfield and this is Officer Mike Phillips," the man said. "Perhaps we should come in," Mayfield said. "We're sorry to disturb you so early in the morning."

"Yeah, sure. Come on in," Eric said. He was still not fully awake. He hoped this had nothing to do with his previous drunk driving incident. He thought that had already been all cleared up.

"Sit down," Eric said, pointing to the sofa. The officers sat uncomfortably while Eric took his place in a big chair. "What's up?"

"Larry and Barbara Carpenter--your parents?" Mayfield questioned.

"You might say that," Eric said cautiously. "I mean...I'm adopted."

"But they raised you," Phillips stated.

"Yeah," Eric agreed.

"Do you know where they were traveling last night?" Mayfield questioned.

"They've been in France, but I imagine they came back to the States, probably flew into Denver if I'm guessing," Eric said.

"They did," Mayfield affirmed. "They rented a car and apparently were driving back to their home here."

"Yeah, so?" Eric said, sudden fear gripping his heart. Something was clearly wrong.

"I'm afraid we have some bad news for you," Phillips said. He looked down at his note pad.

"They were in a car wreck last night west of Denver," Mayfield said. "Larry was driving too fast for the weather conditions. The car hydroplaned in the rain. Fortunately, a doctor was driving not far behind them. He saw the car go off the road and stopped to help--Dr. Roger Mason. He was able to help your father. But your mother had internal injuries." Mayfield paused. Then he said, "Your mother didn't make it. She died at the scene."

"Oh, no...." Eric couldn't speak.

At that moment Darlene entered the room in her bathrobe.

"I heard what you said, Officer," Darlene said. "Eric, I'm so sorry!"

"Are you Eric's wife?" Officer Phillips asked.

"No. I'm his sister," Darlene replied.

"We're sharing this place until she marries her fiancé," Eric added.

"We're very sorry for your loss," Phillips said. "Your father is still in the hospital in Denver, but he is expected to be OK." He was looking at Darlene.

"Oh, Larry isn't my adopted father, only Eric's. I was adopted by another couple," Darlene explained. "But of course, I care about Larry and Barbara...Oh, poor Barbara!"

"We're sorry to have to bring you this news," Mayfield added. "Here are some phone numbers you'll need." Mayfield handed Eric a note paper. It included the name of the hospital room, the coroner's office, and other information they might need.

"You'll find my number there as well," Mayfield said. "Just in case we can be of any help."

"Thank you, Officer," Eric said.

"You're very kind," Darlene added.

The officers excused themselves, got into their grey police unit, and left.

Darlene called her parents and Joe, her fiancé, to tell them what had happened. Bill and Judy came right over to the apartment to offer their support and sympathy. Joe promised to come over to the apartment later that day and asked if he could do anything to help. Eric had called Pastor Glen, and he also came. They all agreed to pray for Larry.

After the visitors had left, Eric told Darlene," I'm going to drive to Denver to see dad at the hospital."

"You don't think you're going alone, do you?" Darlene said.

"You have work," Eric said.

"I'll take a family emergency day," Darlene replied. "I'll call in and we can be on our way."

"Darlene, you don't have to--"

"I'm your sister, Eric. Your twin. Do you think I'd let you go through this alone?"

CHAPTER 20

Eric and Darlene found the hospital room and saw Larry lying in bed with his head bandaged. There was a man they didn't know sitting beside the bed.

"Eric. Darlene. You shouldn't have come here," Larry said. "I'm going to be fine."

"Dad, I wouldn't let you be alone at a time like this," Eric said.

"I'm Dr. Roger Mason," the man said, standing. "I was a witness to the accident."

"You're the man who helped my parents!" Eric exclaimed.

"Well, I did the best I could under the circumstances," Dr. Mason said. The two men shook hands.

"This is my sister Darlene," Eric said.

"We want to thank you for what you did." Darlene said.

Roger nodded in acknowledgement.

"The officers who told us about the wreck said you were with my mother when she died," Eric said. "Did she say anything...at the end?"

"Yes. She asked me if I were a Christian,and I said I was. Then she asked me to pray with her. She prayed the sinner's prayer and accepted Christ as her personal Savior."

"Oh, praise God!!' Darlene exclaimed.

"That's good news! I'm so glad," Eric agreed.

"Her spirit is with Jesus, Eric," Darlene said. "In 2 Corinthians 5:8 Paul says that to be absent from the body is to be present with the Lord."

"Yes, that's right," Dr. Mason agreed.

"That is a great comfort," Eric said.

"Take the church meeting somewhere else," Larry said. "My head hurts bad enough without all that superstition and fairy tale stuff. I don't take well to all this talk about God. If there is a God, He let Barbara die."

"She had severe internal injuries--" Dr. Mason started to explain.

"If there's a God, He could have prevented the accident," Larry argued.

"God gives us free will, Dad," Eric said. "You chose to drive too fast in the rain. The car hydroplaned. That's why you crashed. God had nothing to do with it."

"If there is a God, He could have intervened," Larry insisted. "A good God would intervene and prevent the accident. I can't believe in a God who would let bad things happen. That's why I don't believe there is a God."

"Yes, God could have prevented it. But God usually lets us make our choices--and take the consequences of those choices," Darlene said quietly.

"Well, it's God's fault that my wife is dead, and I am in bad shape," Larry insisted.

"But Dad," Eric said. "Don't blame God. The Lord will help you. Jesus is real. He's alive. And He loves you and wants to save you."

"If you reject Jesus, your spirit will be separated from God forever after you die," Darlene said.

"You mean I'll burn in hell? Well, all my friends will be there, so that's fine with me," Larry said.

"God wants to help you, Larry," Dr. Mason put in.

"You mean well, Doctor, and I thank you for all you've done. But if you're gonna join in on all this Christian stuff, please don't bother me with it. I'll never change my mind about God. There is no God. He doesn't exist and that's that."

"It's your choice, Dad," Eric said. "God gave everyone free will, and He is not going to force anyone to accept Him."

"I think maybe your dad needs rest now," Dr. Mason said. "Perhaps later he would discuss his spiritual condition."

Turning to Larry, Dr. Mason said, "God does love you and He does want a relationship with you. But we are going to leave now and let you rest. I'm going to leave a little booklet for you to read when you feel up to it." Roger placed a small book on the table beside Larry's bed.

"What is it?" Larry asked.

"How to become a Christian and live a life for Christ," Dr. Mason replied.

"Trash," Larry said. "Don't bother me with trash like that."

Then the doctor and the young people left the room. As they proceeded down the hall. they did not see Larry make an obscene gesture with his right hand as he watched them leave.

As they walked down the hall, Eric asked, "Dr. Mason, do you know when my dad can leave the hospital?"

"No. You'd have to ask the physician who's caring for him here. I'd guess it will some time yet. I'm sorry we upset him. I didn't know how he felt about being a Christian."

"I'm glad you were here. We are grateful for your help, Doctor," Eric said.

"To be very candid, Eric, your dad isn't out of the woods. He still has to have surgery on that fractured leg. If I can be of any help, let me know." He gave a card with his phone number on it to Eric. "You and your father will be in my prayers."

"Thank you again for all you did. You were a stranger, but you treated us just like family," Darlene said.

“We’re all the family of God, Eric,” Dr. Mason said.

“Well, you were a Good Samaritan,” Dalene declared.

“We can all be Good Samaritans in our daily lives,” the doctor said. “As we share the love of Christ.”

After the doctor left, Darlene and Eric called Pastor Glen and asked him to join them in praying for Larry. Darlene called Joe and asked him to pray, as well.

CHAPTER 21

BEFORE LARRY WAS TO GO into surgery, Darlene and Eric came into his room and prayed for him. Larry was groggy from pre-surgery drugs, but he heard them.

"You still believe in your fairy tales," he said. "When will you two grow up?"

"We believe God wants to heal you and we are praying that the surgery will go well. We are praying for the surgeon and the nurses--and everyone involved in your care."

"Look, if I'm gonna die, I'm gonna die. And that's the end. There's nothin' after that."

"But, Dad, the Bible teaches--"

"You know I don't believe the Bible. Now leave me alone," Larry said.

"It would be best if you left now," a nurse in the corner of the room said, stepping forward. Eric and Darlene left.

"He doesn't know what he's saying," Darlene defended. "It's the drugs speaking."

"You're trying to be kind, Darlene," Eric said. "But he knows what he's saying. He's always had that attitude."

The next day Larry was recovering well. Eric and Darlene spent time with Larry before returning to the motel for the night.

Early the next morning Eric's phone rang. It was the hospital calling with bad news. Larry had suffered a post-surgery stroke. The nurse on the phone suggested that Eric come immediately to the hospital, as Larry's condition was critical.

When Darlene and Eric's went into the hospital room, his bed was still in an upright position where he'd been sitting. A nurse came in and gently explained that Larry had passed away just a few minutes earlier. Eric and Darlene sat down to take time to absorb the news, each lost in thought and prayer.

On the edge of the bed, there was the booklet that Dr. Mason had left. Larry had apparently been reading it.

"Eric, I think your dad was reading this booklet, or maybe he had read it. Maybe he prayed and asked God to forgive his sins," Darlene said. "Maybe he committed his life to Christ before he died."

"I hope so," Eric said. "Anyway, his life is over now. There's nothing we can do."

On their way back home, Darlene said, "Your parents would want you to take good care of yourself. And I'm going to help you do just that. You should see your doctor again soon."

"I'll make an appointment," Eric promised.

"No matter what happens, Eric, I'm your twin sister. I will never leave you. I will take care of you."

"But I want you to get married and have your own home with your husband. You deserve your own life, a happy life, no matter what happens to me," Eric said.

"I am going to get married. And Joe and I will have a home of our own. But I will always be here to take care of you whenever you need me," Darlene said. "You and I have a strong bond. Nothing can sever it. I am going to stay by your side no matter what. I have already talked to Joe about it. He wouldn't have it any other way. He will support me as strongly as I will support you. We're family and that's what we do."

"I am hoping God will heal me," Eric said. "I want to study and become a preacher. And I want to marry Eleanor," he mused.

"Eleanor Chase is a wonderful girl. You should ask her to marry you soon," Darlene advised.

"I plan to," Eric said.

"I believe God is going to heal you and give you a new lease on life," Darlene said. "You can be a witness to many people for Christ. I was just thinking today you have so much good material for sermons. When I was in the hospital, my dad told me I'd had a blood transfusion, and it saved my life. As you know, there are four blood types. A person has to receive his or her correct blood type from the donor. For instance, if you're Type A positive and I'm Type B, you can't receive my blood. But if you're also Type A positive, I can be the donor for you. The unusual thing is that a person with Type 0 blood can give to anyone regardless of their type. Anyone can receive Type 0 blood. Type 0 is called the universal donor."

"You learned all that in nursing school?"

"Yes, and from my dad because he's a doctor,," Darlene said.

"So I see where you're going with this for a sermon," Eric said. "Jesus is the Universal Donor. His blood can be applied to anyone for forgiveness of sons. Jesus is a Type 0 donor, so to speak."

"Yes, you could give a good sermon on that concept," Darlene said.

"Well, of course, you'd help me," Eric declared.

"Of course! Oh, Eric, I feel sure the Lord is going to use you in His work. You have a love for people, and you want to see them saved."

"Yes. I think we are living in the end times. People need to turn to Jesus," Eric declared.

"Eric, I had an unusual experience a couple of weeks ago," Darlene said. "I was just about to fall asleep one night. I was thinking of nothing, really. Just almost asleep--when a sudden thought struck me, as if someone was speaking to me, although it was not an audible voice. I believe it was the Lord giving me a message. The thought that came into my mind was: 'The rapture is imminent.' I usually don't use the word 'imminent.' I know what it means. It means that something is just about to happen; it's pending."

"That's right," Eric agreed. "I believe the Lord was giving you a message. We need to be ready for His return. When He ascended into heaven, as told in the book of Acts, an angel told those who were watching Him go up into heaven that Jesus would return in the same manner. And we know from His own words that He will return. He gave certain signs to look for. Those signs tell us He could return any time."

"So His return could be today, tomorrow, next week, next month, a year from now--"

"Or in five years from now, or ten years, or a hundred," Eric broke in. "No one knows the day or hour our Lord will return. But we are told in His word to watch and be ready. I think that His return is soon, or imminent. We should live as if He would return today but also carry on His work, not knowing how long it will be before He returns," Eric stated.

"Yes," Darlene agreed. "In Matthew 24:42, Jesus said, 'Watch therefore for ye know not what hour your Lord doth come.'"

"That is what we must keep in mind," Eric affirmed.

"You can give sermons to help people prepare for His return," Darlene said. "I feel sure God will heal you and give you the time you need to serve him."

"Yes. The Lord has been so good to me. And I am believing Him for healing. I want to lead others to know Christ. One thing is sure. There is only one <u>true</u> Replacement Son."

"What do you mean, Eric? I know you were a replacement son, but you're grown now; and you can put your childhood behind you."

"What I mean is, Jesus Christ was sent by God to replace us, to take the punishment we should have taken for our sins--death! Death on the cross! He replaced me," Eric said. "He was my substitute! The punishment for sin is death; but God allowed Christ to take the punishment for us--so if we accept His gift, we can be saved as we trust in Him," Eric said. "Christ, the Substitute, the Replacement Son. He took our place on the cross. He died instead of us sinners. I always thought of a replacement son meaning a child born after the death of a previous child, to take the place of the dead child. But in this case, the Child took the death of the sinner who would then be able live by accepting salvation through Christ's atonement. God demands that sin be punished by death. So Christ stepped up and died instead of the sinner--so the sinner could have eternal life through faith in what Christ did for him at the cross."

"Yes, Jesus took the place of the sinner on the cross--a substitute or replacement--taking the punishment the sinner should have taken. In doing so, He purchased the redemption for all who would believe and follow Him. So, it's like we as sinners were condemned to death but Christ stepped in and said, 'I am here to take your place.' He had no sin, so He could be the sacrifice for our sins--the Lamb of God. It is as if He told the executioner, 'Stop! Do not execute this prisoner. I am here to set him free. I am here to take his place. Execute me, instead. I am the substitute. I am the replacement.' Eric, I think you should preach a sermon the 'The True Replacement Son,' Darlene said. "It would help people see what Christ did for us.:

"I believe God is going to heal me and I am going to become a minister and preach sermons like that," Eric declared. "But I can say, like Paul said in Romans 14, verse 8, whether we live or whether we die, it is in Him."

"That is true," Darlene agreed. In the first chapter of Philippians, Verse 21 through 24, Paul wrote: 'For me to live is Christ, and to die is gain. But if I live in the flesh, this is the fruit of my labour; yet what I shall chose I wot not. For I am in a strait betwixt two, having a desire to depart, and be with Christ, which is far better. Nevertheless, to abide in the flesh is more needful for you.'"

"But whatever happens, as long as I have breath, I will urge people to turn their lives over to Jesus," Eric affirmed.

After they returned to their apartment, the first thing they did was to pray together.

THE END

EPILOGUE

TWO YEARS LATER:

Eric's latest physical exams revealed he was in perfect health. Scans showed no sign of a tumor. He and Darlene gave God the glory for healing, Eric married Eleanor Chase, the girl he'd worked with at the hardware store. They planned a June wedding. Eric was working to complete Bible College and was already giving sermons at various churches. His plan was to travel with a missionary team to preach the gospel and distribute Bibles overseas.

Darlene and Joe O'Casey married, and Darlene had baby girl.

Dr. Bill and Judy Simms, Darlene's parents, continued to enjoy a relationship with Darlene and Eric.

Jacqueline Baker, the birth mother, continued to enjoy a relationship with Darlene and Eric. They eventually met her husband, Wayne Tompson, a very nice man. Darlene and Eric also enjoyed a relationship with the Bakers' children, Jerry and Linda.

Robert Carlson, the natural father of Darlene and Eric, had entered college right after high school. When he was a sophomore, he raped a young woman. He also tried to kill her. There was a witness. Robert was convicted of rape. He was sent to prison. He remained there.

James and Helen Baker, Jacqueline's parents, learned about Eric and Darlene and were glad their daughter had refused to have an abortion when she was sixteen.

Pastor Glen continued to work with the church and with young people.

Dr. Stanley Fisher continued to deliver babies at the hospital where Bill Simms, Darlene's father, continued to work.

Nancy Pierce's conscience bothered. She confessed to Eric and Darlene her role in changing the birth certificates. She gave them $2,000, the amount Larry had paid for the false certificates. She asked forgiveness, and they forgave her.

Dr. Roger Mason and his wife Sharon continued to help others through their work and their church.

Officer Alex Mayfield and Officer Mike Phillips continued to work in law enforcement, Mayfield being promoted to Chief of Police and Phillips being offered a position with the F.B.I.

Printed in the United States
by Baker & Taylor Publisher Services